strangers' gate

strangers' gate

tom casey

a tom doherty associates book
new york

STRANGERS' GATE

Copyright © 2006 by Tom Casey

This book is printed on acid-free paper.

A Forge Book
Published by Tom Doherty Associates, LLC
175 Fifth Avenue
New York, NY 10010

www.tor.com

Forge® is a registered trademark of Tom Doherty Associates, LLC.

Library of Congress Cataloging-in-Publication Data

Casey, Tom.
    Strangers' gate / Tom Casey.—1st ed.
        p.   cm.
    "A Tom Doherty Associates book."
    ISBN-13: 978-0-765-31190-0
    ISBN-10: 0-765-31190-9
        1. Air pilots—Fiction.   2. Caribbean area—Fiction.   I. Title.
    PS3553.A79363S77   2006
    813'.54—dc22
                                                    2005033728

First Edition: June 2006

Printed in the United States of America

0 9 8 7 6 5 4 3 2 1

For Gail Fly

He understood that men are forever strangers to one another, that no one ever comes really to know anyone, that imprisoned in the dark womb of our mother we come to life without having seen her face, that we are given to her arms a stranger, and that caught in the insoluble prison of being, we escape it never, no matter what arms may clasp us, what mouth may kiss us, what heart may warm us, never, never, never, never, never.

—Thomas Wolfe

part one

The days of our love
Ever pouring pure water
Into pure water.

—Chuck Tripi

Why was he here? Why was he always, more or less,
here? He would have been glad of a mirror, to ask
himself that question.

—Malcolm Lowry

one

I knew this was the end for Margo and me. She was having an affair. In a way it was a relief; we'd been moving toward divorce for some time.

Loving Margo had always been difficult, like learning to write with your left hand for no sensible reason. Our emotions were always in a tangle and I was tired of thinking it was my fault. We'd agreed to work on our problems, but privately I had stopped believing in the worth of continuing to try. I felt empty, hurting like a man with a missing leg who feels pain in a phantom limb.

Our differences were fundamental: Margo is a workaholic; I'm more of a dreamer. She's a joiner; I prefer the comforts of solitude. Margo has fixed notions about life, with that need to be right about everything: to her the world is black and white, clean and geometric, a solvable equation; for me it's a barely articulate asylum of howls, a mess of misconceptions and delusions. In the beginning, these differences didn't seem to matter. Relationships defy prediction; ours wasn't terrible; over time we had become accommodating spouses, but I was tired of accommodation. My move to St. Croix was the last straw; she didn't understand any of it. Now I had to return home to face whatever there was to face, which included a long-planned vacation in Paris I was no longer eager to take.

The flight from Miami to JFK was full, so I flew to Boston instead and took the Acela train down to New York. All things considered, it was the fastest option available.

I normally find train travel restful, but not this time. A man across the aisle had been annoying me by turning pages of a magazine; he was not reading at all, just turning the pages one after another in a frantic way, making them snap audibly. He had a stack of other magazines on the seat beside him, so this was bound to go on for some time. A man behind me was talking loudly on a cell phone about his cancer; a young mother in front of me was yelling at her whining child. I had a seat to myself and any move would be an uncomfortable invasion of some other traveler's privacy, so I was stuck with these distractions. Other people sometimes make you doubt your humanity.

I turned to look out the window, where homes in suburban neighborhoods went into and out of my view. The rhythm of the rails was a kind of clock. Dusk was finished. Time was passing in the lives of people I didn't know. Time was passing in my own life. With my head against the window, I noticed my transparent reflection, a Siamese twin of myself superimposed over the passing scene, staring at me. In the reflected background I saw the image of the man and his magazines, his ghost, so it seemed, madly turning pages, searching for some answer to his life. With this thought, staring into the eyes of my own ghostly reflection, I was unable to imagine myself in his world; I had escaped all that.

But I was never really of that world. In my heart, I'm a pilot more than anything else. Purpose is wedded to flight mysteriously. Sometimes flying is a form of secular prayer, a way to see secret places in the world and in the spirit; sometimes it is the mere childlike delight of audacity, delight that pertains to pride as a test of skill. You are what you do, how you dream. Maybe at the end I was, as Margo said, flying away from her, but she never understood it as more than that.

Airplanes have been more in the nature of a necessity for me; I was around them growing up; my father was a pilot who believed that learning to fly was the path to self-confidence; his stepsister, my aunt Madeline, a large influence in my life, was an air-show stunt pilot who opened me up to early flying experiences. After her husband, who was also a show pilot, was killed in a crash, she retired from the circuit. But when I was a boy she took me up in her biplane to show me snap rolls and spins. I learned to fly in high school.

After college, the Air Force rounded out my aviation experience with the chance to fly high-performance jets. In my Air Force days I discovered the afterburner's high thrill: when you're alone for the first time in a supersonic jet the world makes complete sense. I like stimulation and respond well to risk; it must have been obvious to my superiors; they joked about my genial nature on the ground and aggressive manner in the air. As a fighter pilot I was schooled in small-arms combat, escape and evasion, and psychological survival. It seemed like a game to me then, but it was, after all, very serious, and a day would come when that training proved useful.

After a year and a half of active duty, I got my reserve assignment flying the F-16 and became a weekend warrior: Lt. Jason Walker, call sign "Double-T." Our squadron was a collegial assortment of testosterone alpha types: lawyers, airline pilots, and other masters of the universe. We were a modern knighthood, the Officers' Club resembling a loosely ordered Round Table. In peacetime it was an exalted form of play. We flew fighter formations over New Jersey one weekend each month, slow rolls at Mach 1, fast dashes up the coast for cheeseburgers in Maine. I stayed with it for ten years, until work and time constraints forced me to resign. But flying has always been my antidepressant; I sorely missed it.

That's why before I married Margo I bought a classic Twin Beech 18 to fly. When I needed distance from the routine of my life to make decisions that would change it, I went traveling alone in the Beechcraft. The Beech 18 is a Harley-Davidson of the air, with two big round motors and a twin tail; it's a pilot's plane, and like the Fantail or the Electra Glide, it embodies a dream.

I found my gem in Florida, a customs seizure. Shining in the sun her profile was impressive, but her logbooks read like a rap sheet. I asked around about her. "She's a whore in a white dress," a mechanic warned. But I was in love. I made a low bid and won: she was mine. We got off to a rocky start, however: the left engine failed on the first flight, shattering illusions. So it's going to be like this, I thought. I meant to make this airplane my ally: six months later she had two new engines and a mirror bright finish. Since then we've had an understanding.

When my metropolitan life began to lose purpose, I wandered from it by air. One autumn, almost on a whim, I flew north to Alaska. Alaska is a state of mind, a place of rebirth where self-reliance counts for everything. The northern sun falls thinly on its ice and granite like a failure of faith; in that icy light there are sights so stupendous that all of what you thought you knew about splendor is changed forever. It is beauty with death as its truth; you greet it with caution and wonder. Perhaps the cockpit of an airplane is the only fit seat for these harrowing flirtations.

Beryl Markham was my aunt Madeline's role model. Author, pioneer aviator, and the first person to fly solo from east to west across the Atlantic Ocean, Markham, a beautiful and bold woman, understood that something sacred but perishable had been given to us as the gift of flight. She wrote: "After this era of great pilots is gone . . . it will be found, I think, that all the science of flying has been captured in the breadth of an instrument board, but not the religion of it."

Looking back, I had traveled to Alaska aware that some defining event was imminent; I had wished for it; I had flown across the country following impulse to greet it. This was my Chautauqua. It took four days of flying to reach Emerald Lake, about an hour southeast of Anchorage. As I drew closer to my destination, an emotion akin to what a mountain climber feels facing a summit grew in me; I did not know how my challenge would come, but I seemed to be certain it would.

two

The airplane had been running smoothly all day. I had been flying since morning. When I crossed the last ridge I could see a small dirt airstrip on the far side of a wide glacial lake; mountains were reflected on the glassy water like some colossal thought the earth was having. I banked gently and made an approach along the shoreline. Touchdown was like awakening from a dream.

Later at the cabin, I stood at the water's edge skipping stones on its surface, the ripples describing perfect expanding circles. It's a small miracle among many you acknowledge with agnostic reverence, thinking, You have flown in your plane to be in this place in order to understand something; your silence is the land's silence; your heartbeat is the heartbeat of the earth.

I had been alone on the lake for nearly a week. The weather had been mild, but now heavy snow began to fall. Ready to enjoy the storm, I had cut wood in the afternoon and stacked it on the porch. Earlier the silence was profound; now the wind was up. I had finished stoking the fire and was sitting in my chair with a whiskey when brisk knocking at the door brought me abruptly out of a doze. With annoyance and mild paranoia, I got up and answered.

A woman stood before me: she had Asian features, dark eyes, and sun-browned skin, smooth, not weathered; she pulled back her hood and her hair was jet-black.

"My son is ill," she said. "He has a fever."

"Come in."

I stepped aside and closed the door after her. There was no pretension, no waste of message, in her simple declarative manner.

"Have you called a doctor?"

"There is no doctor. They said to bring him to Anchorage. I tried, but the road is blocked with snow. The men in town know your plane. They told me to come here and that you would take us."

I stared at her without responding. To go aloft was unthinkable; the wind was whipping through the mountains and across the black freezing waters of the inlet. We looked at each other.

"Will you help me?" Her eyes were adamant with petition.

The scale of her request took your breath away, but in the north survival depends on cooperation. This woman was a mother acting according to her nature; it would do no good to go against it. You can tell a storm's coming by a restlessness you feel.

"The storm is just beginning," I said. "There's nothing to be done tonight."

"He's very sick."

"We'll have to wait."

"You'll help me?" It was clear that she was willing to sacrifice her life—and surely she was willing to sacrifice mine—to do what she had to do for her boy.

"I'll do what I can tomorrow. Meet me at the plane when the snow stops."

"Thank you," she said, nodding her head to the bargain as she pulled on her hood.

When she was gone I had that heavy sense of Fate's offering me this challenge as an alternative to some accident that hadn't happened yet.

The next afternoon the snow was still falling, but it was lighter. I walked to the airstrip. She was waiting for me.

"Where's your boy?"

"With my sister. Until we are ready."

I dug the plane out and cleaned snow from the wings and cleared the runway with a log dragged behind her truck. She was with me the whole while. By the time we finished, the snow had stopped, but the sky was unsettled and the wind was howling in the tops of the trees. I looked at the airplane, trying to get a feeling for the flight we were about to make.

"You'd better get your son," I told her. She drove off.

I don't believe in mysticism, but I do believe that we exist in a relationship with machines that seems mystical at times; they develop personalities that are echoes of our own, reflecting the care or lack of care we give them, and they speak to us in a language of rhythms. When you fly north in October, it's always tricky and you have to worry about icing. It takes experience and skill, and luck is also important if you have enough of it to count on. Looking at the darkening sky, I had a bad feeling. Snow began to fall again; I could not see the mountains. I did not trust this weather and it was obvious we'd have to fly at night.

I got the engines started and they were rumbling evenly. It was a familiar and satisfying sensation to feel the plane alive again. In a little while the truck returned. I left the engines running and set the brakes and went back through the cabin to help her climb on board. She held the boy tightly against the prop wash. Once they were aboard I locked the hatch behind her and led her up front. I put her in the seat next to mine in the cockpit. The boy was zippered into her coat now, asleep at her breast. Her face was determined; I didn't see any fear in it.

"Is your lap belt tight enough?" I asked. She looked down at her waist, rechecked it, and nodded.

Twilight was gone; it was dark. I felt for the flashlight I keep in a pouch behind the seat, ready if I needed it, and I had a penlight in my shirt pocket. I checked the compass against the GPS and reset the directional gyro; then I set the flaps.

"Are you ready?"

I taxied to the end of the airstrip. Once aligned, I turned on the electric fuel boost pumps, started the clock, locked the tail wheel, and eased the throttles to full power. The engines roared in the darkness. As the plane began to roll, a keen state of alertness made time seem to slow down. I felt the wheels tug left and right as we crashed a path through varying depths of snow; my feet worked the rudder pedals to hold the takeoff heading; it was critically important to keep the plane tracking straight. When I felt the translation of weight shift from wheels to wing I eased back on the control wheel and the plane lifted into the air. I counted three seconds and retracted the landing gear.

We were climbing normally through three thousand feet and I was settling into the flight, just beginning to feel comfortable, when a snapping and popping sound, and then a flash, was followed by a smell of burning wires; the cockpit went black; something had shorted and very bad news quickly dawned: we had complete electrical failure. I feared a fire and felt for the fire extinguisher under my seat. Then I took the penlight out of my pocket and turned it on so I could see the instruments. The gyros, airspeed, and altimeter were okay, and the non–electric engine instruments were fine; everything else read zero. I got the larger flashlight and handed it to the woman to hold on the panel. Our situation was fragile; we were in the weather without radios, with no means of navigation, no means of making an approach; I had only the compass and a clock.

"Are you all right?" I asked.

She nodded. If she felt fearful, it was buried under resolve. Her expression was concentrated.

Anchorage was an hour away. I put the chart in her lap and traced our course with my finger. There are two runways at Anchorage that run east and west and extend nearly to the water.

We climbed safely above the mountains, but we were still in the clouds. I accelerated to cruise speed. I figured an elapsed time to Anchorage and subtracted ten minutes for the descent. I did the arithmetic and tried to convince myself that dead reckoning was a time-honored skill. Once past the mountains I could descend over the water, to just above sea level if necessary, aiming for the airport until shoreline lights should appear in snow or fog. I had no other ideas.

The woman realized we had a new problem before I did: "Do you have other batteries?"

I didn't. The larger flashlight was dimming rapidly, failing like life in mortal illness. I took the penlight out of my pocket and gave it to her. "Turn it off and count to twenty, then turn it on again for three seconds, then off for twenty, and keep doing it." She nodded.

Holding her sleeping child tightly against her breast, she held the light on the instruments, then switched it off. I was amazed at the absolute darkness. I could only hold the control wheel in my hand and feel for pitch or roll and listen for a change in the rush of air that would indicate a shift in speed.

We flew on. I went into myself to find inside something I needed to get through this. If you took comfort in what was familiar about flight—the steady howl of wind across the wing, the throb of the engines, the feel of flight controls, the chill air biting your face—you could keep confidence from collapsing. If you took comfort in these things and did not calculate your chances of surviving through the next hour, or rationalize impact as at least swift death, or try to remember your happiest time in this life, then it was all right. It was all right if you didn't think. But panic wore different disguises just below the surface of calm. You could feel it as swollen regret that you had ever answered the door or left the cabin where you had come to think; you could feel it as a change in heart from sympathy for the stranger and her child to wishing with utter despair that your life had been left undisturbed. But the reality was that Fate had come knocking, death was beside you, this was the situation, and there was no virtue, nothing like valor in any of it. You could move through the panic and keep it down by making it become a swelling in the throat, or a sick feeling in the gut, because you could keep those under control. You could do anything but let the panic out. If the panic came out, it was over, so you might as well keep calm for as long as the light could blink for three seconds in every twenty. So you listened to the engines, and felt for the propeller controls, and made slight adjustments in the dark to keep them in sync. It didn't break your heart so much if you stopped wondering what your life added up to, whether the days and years had any significance or effect or if it meant anything. You thought about the relief when this trial would be over. You thought about the cup of coffee you'd drink thoughtfully when you were alone again. You thought about the child who would live and about the mother who would have a story to tell about heroism that was only hers. And you thought about everything that was working out so far and that maybe you had luck. You still had time to make the right choices. Time can be a friend, but it can also turn against you, mocking your squandering of it before running out. The sound

of smoothly running engines brought solace in the dark as minutes passed and these thoughts came and went.

When I calculated that we were forty miles south of Anchorage, I
felt safe believing I could drop down to a lower altitude and
drive up the channel. That way I'd surely see lights and find my
way to the airport, or land as best I might on the shoreline.

I began to descend.

The penlight didn't show any sign of dimming, and I was
thankful for that. Our speed was two and a half miles per
minute. We went through three thousand feet, and then two
thousand, and then one thousand, and when we flew below five
hundred feet I told her to leave the light on steadily and shine it
directly on the instruments. I continued down, watching the altitude closely. I had been able to maintain a fierce mental pitch
to immunize us against peril, but that high level of concentration
was fading fast. I leveled at three hundred feet and saw nothing.
I went to two hundred feet, nothing. By my time estimate we
should be closing on the shoreline. At one hundred feet above
the ocean I was beginning to get fearful. By my calculations
we were too low to fly blind much longer.

I was about to pull up when suddenly a light appeared below
us! The light shone as a dim fuzzy glow in the darkness, but it
extinguished. We were in thick fog. My heart fell when I lost it,
but another reappeared almost immediately, went out, and a
third appeared again. The three lights were flashing in a line to
the right, but I was not aligned and flew beyond them, and they
were gone. They were not beacons, I thought; they were flashing
lights, lights flashing in sequence, *sequenced flashing lights for a
runway! Could it be?* Calm down; calm down. I passed the lights
at nearly a ninety-degree angle, so I would have to maneuver
immediately to pick them up again.

"Hold the light right here!" I told the woman, indicating the artificial horizon and the altimeter. She watched my face. I put the plane into a twenty-five-degree left bank. At my present indicated speed, that bank angle would reverse my course in sixty seconds. If I held that bank for an additional forty-five seconds, then flew straight, I should be on a course that would carry me over the lights again at a better intercept angle. I was very low, below a hundred feet above the water, no room for error. I held the controls with iron concentration and began to count out loud to sixty. One, two, three—the altimeter needle didn't budge. The bank was at exactly twenty-five degrees—fifty-nine, sixty. I held the bank and started a second count to forty-five. This maneuver should put me on an intercept course, but it was at best an educated guess.

The whole experience felt unreal, like something being imagined—forty-four, forty-five. I leveled the wings. Figuring the timed turn had positioned me to within twenty seconds of the lights, I began another count. It was astounding: the sequenced flasher had been given and taken away, offered but withdrawn, a gift, but one to be earned. If I could find it again, follow it to a runway, and land . . . it seemed impossible . . . but then, off to the left, *I picked up the lights!* My course was near perfect, drifting me slowly over to them. It was miraculous! As I approached the lights, I made a slight turn to track down the center of their sequenced guidance, being careful not to climb or descend.

But again Fate withdrew its offer: *the lights vanished.* The runway approach lights, the centerline and edge lights I should expect to materialize, did not. Instead, the last sequenced flasher passed under the nose and we were once again alone in the black darkness. I didn't understand it. I got furious. *If I am a plaything of some demonic force, so be it, but I am going to win at this: believe your instincts—those were lead-in lights; therefore, a runway exists. Even if it was invisible for reasons unknown, there must exist a runway in front of me in the dark.*

I held the compass heading and once again began to count—twelve seconds, eleven, ten, nine—I reached for the landing gear lever and moved it to the down position, being careful not to change altitude.

Nothing happened.

Of course nothing happened: the gear is electrically actuated—five, four—I kicked up a protective cover hinged over the emergency gear extension pedal near my right foot and slammed it with the heel of my boot. The wheels dropped with a thud. I felt for the hand crank at my right side, pulled it out and pushed it forward a quarter turn to engage the downlock—two, one—and now I squeezed off the power, walking the throttles back gently and slowly, holding the nose up while the speed decreased. When it reached landing speed, I added enough power to let the plane drift down, holding a vertical velocity of 150 feet per minute, a seaplane technique for landing on glassy water when you can't judge your height above the surface. It was all I could think of to do. The runway had to be there, reason whispered. It had to be.

And it was. We hit the ground blind and bounced; I threw the control wheel forward; we hit the ground again, but this time I kept us from bouncing with forward elevator pressure, and we were rolling. We rolled in the darkness; I held the heading and let the aircraft slow without the brakes, fearing that an uneven application would make us swerve off the pavement. The plane rolled to a stop.

We were down. We were safe.

I pulled the fuel mixtures to idle cutoff and the engines quit. It was over. For long minutes I was unable to speak.

"Stay here," I said at last. "I'll go for help."

I went back through the cabin and got out and walked along the runway perimeter in the fog and found the fire station. The

sign said: Anchorage International. I knocked on the door, sur-
prising the firemen on duty. They were playing cards at a table
behind the trucks. One of the men got up and came to the door
and opened it. The others watched.

"I've just landed," I told him. "I've got a woman with a sick
child."

"But the airport's closed," he said. "How did you land?"

I told them briefly what had happened and they jumped up
from their game and took me back to the airplane in a green
and yellow emergency vehicle. The fog was thick and bright
against their headlights; little was visible. The plane material-
ized in front of us like a dark vision in a deeply felt dream.

After the woman and her boy were safely on their way I
learned that the airport had been closed for fog, but someone
forgot to turn off the sequenced flashers. That was my luck, but
it was a hard road to it.

I learned later that the boy had tularemia. Rabbit fever. It's
rare. It comes on suddenly with a high temperature, stomach
pain, skin rash, and other nasty symptoms. The doctors said he
had twelve hours to live. It's bacterial, so when they shot him up
with antibiotics everything was all right.

Our problem had a simple cause: a lead running from the
right generator got loose and grounded against the cowling,
sending a short to the voltage regulator, melting it, disabling the
battery, and knocking out the left generator in the process, re-
sulting in complete loss of electrical power.

"You fly like someone with a death wish," one of the firemen
said when he heard my story.

"A life wish, actually," I told him. "Sometimes you don't have
options; you do the best you can and hope the outcome's worth
the risk."

three

I sat on the Acela train remembering that Alaskan adventure as something sacred to the story of my life. It defined the direction my life would take after returning. The train crossed a bridge beside a bay and I could see a church steeple above the trees of a small town on the far side. So peaceful, I thought. A simple life has eluded me. Divorce would further complicate it.

Marriages end for different reasons. With Margo and me there was no single ugly event I could point to; rather, our failure was founded on small inattentions. To me it seemed as if a thread had been pulled some time ago and the cloth of marriage had frayed and slowly come undone.

In New York there is an entrance to Central Park called Strangers' Gate. Other gates honor the guilds, but Strangers' Gate pays tribute to all. We often climbed its stone steps together to the promenades, paths, and park greens where the nameless and faceless had identity, where people could connect. But Margo and I were strangers now. When I climbed the steps these days I went alone, and the gate seemed less a welcome than a prophecy.

Over the years we had fallen into avoidance strategies: Margo withdrew into work, and I, when I wasn't working, withdrew into books and into flying. We ignored our growing problem: Margo hates failure and I hate imposition; procrastination kept us together.

Before the stock market crash, I had been a marketing executive in a number of dot-com firms during the expansion of the Internet. It was an exciting time. People knew something big was happening, and my job was to show them how to buy into it. Deals were done in minutes. Vast sums were spent on the assumption that the wired were connected to a new invincible age.

The technology was constantly evolving and the flood of money added to the excitement. Two of the companies I was involved with took off; one was sold privately, and one went public in the same month. I was done. At the age of forty-one, I retired with a modest fortune and began to think about what I wanted to do with the rest of my life. Whatever course I set, airplanes would be a part of it. As it turned out, my experience in the Beech 18 led to a chance to fly airboats in St. Croix. It was a dream job for someone who didn't need one, but I'm getting ahead of my story.

four

The Acela raced past New London toward New York.

Blaming your spouse for the breakdown of a marriage is a futile, unworthy, and ultimately dishonest exercise. If Margo was having an affair it could be in response to one I'd had. She and I had begun to fight on a regular basis, one pretext or another growing into shouts, slamming doors, disappointed silence. All grasses were greener when I met Charlotte Lansing and her dreadful husband, Alan, for the first time on New Year's Eve two years before my move to St. Croix. Margo introduced us.

We had been invited to a party on East 63rd Street, in a town house near Fifth Avenue. Margo and I cabbed to the Oak Bar at the Plaza Hotel for a preparty cocktail. A light snow was falling when the taxi dropped us in front. The gilt entry of the Plaza was bustling with well-dressed guests, and that night Central

Park had a wintry grandeur identical to images of old New York embellishing the murals inside.

We walked around the Palm Court to the right, past the lobby to the Oak Bar, where we got a table right away. This was fortunate; the room was packed. We ordered our drinks and I was about to say something when a voice behind me cried out above the din: "Margo!" I turned toward the voice.

A couple two tables away were waving. I didn't recognize them. Margo smiled and waved back.

"Who are they?" I asked.

"Alan and Charlotte Lansing."

"Who's Alan Lansing?"

"He's a partner with G&LJ Capital. Investment bankers. Our firm has had business with them from time to time. Shall I invite them over?"

"Sure."

The clamor made it impossible to communicate without yelling. Margo leaned forward and mouthed, *Would you like to join us?* They nodded, and when the waiter returned with our drinks we were a foursome.

"We're on our way to a party on Sixty-third Street," Margo said.

"The Meekers?" Alan said.

"You're going, too?" Margo asked.

"Jim and I ran into each other at an auction last month," he said, with a hint of Locust Valley Lockjaw.

If something in Alan seemed unctuous, my first impression of his wife was strong and positive. She had very white, nearly perfect teeth and smooth soft skin tinted with a winter tan. Her eyes were green, highlighted by an emerald necklace and platinum blond hair pulled back tightly into a braided bun. Her overall style was bold and smart. I didn't make the connection at the time, but with her black brocade pants and a black bolero jacket her chic resembled in more than a few ways my aunt Madeline's aviator élan.

"When did you and Margo meet?" I said.

"Last spring, at a—"

"—I'm sorry," I interrupted her when my foot accidentally touched hers under the table.

"No, that was me," she said.

We smiled together at the silliness of awkward accidents.

"Margo and I met at a charity function during the spring. Some cause or other; I forget."

"Do you know the Meekers very well?"

"Not too. We have so many acquaintances." She shrugged slightly. "Life revolves around Alan's business relationships."

"What sort of work does he do?"

"Investments. Investment banking. Venture capital."

Her tone was unenthused. I wondered if it was general boredom with her husband or something else.

"I'm so sick of Christmas," I said, changing the subject.

"Wasn't yours merry?" She smiled.

"I mean the hype. It's absurd. These days people string up colored lights after Labor Day."

"It decorates their unhappiness," she said.

I was about to respond when Alan turned my way suddenly, crashing into the rapport growing between his wife and me: "Margo mentioned that you're in the Internet world. Which aspect?"

"Search engines," I told him, hoping to drop the subject.

"I'm interested."

"We're working from several directions to come up with a comprehensive indexing model."

"I'd like to hear more about it when you've got the time."

I'm sure you would, I thought. I smiled and deployed an evasive tactic: "Happy New Year," I said, holding forth my glass. All raised glasses in a toast.

"Happy New Year."

I noticed Charlotte's eyes on me as she sipped her wine.

"So what big deals are you working on, Alan?" Margo asked. He began to talk about a logging company in the Northwest. I lost the thread of their conversation, happy to turn my attention once again to Charlotte.

"Have you always lived in New York?"

"I grew up in Greenwich; I moved here after college to work on Wall Street."

"Is that where you met Alan?"

"We met through mutual friends. My specialty was tax-free municipal bonds, boring but safe."

"You don't seem boring or safe." The words were out before I realized they were rash. She smiled again.

"Are you still working?" I said.

"I left the firm after we married. Alan wanted me to stay home. I kept my interest in the market; I've got a knack; at least I like to think I do."

She didn't look like a creature from the money trade; she looked like a print ad for jewels, a finely cut and polished gem. Beneath her poise I sensed restlessness—she fidgeted with her wedding diamond and frequently surveyed the room; I wondered if she was happy.

"I grew up in Rye," I told her. "We were neighbors; maybe we've met."

"Did you know . . . ," and she offered a few names, one I knew, who had been a bartender at a place called Boodles, where I had once seen the infamous attorney Roy Cohn romancing a cluster of gay bikers, and a radio personality in his drinking days insulting everyone in earshot.

"My father lost his job when I was in high school," she told me. "Greenwich is a bad place to be poor. It made me more aware of money as a shield against all the things that can happen when you don't have it."

"Money can't buy happiness, but I guess it buys a lot of freedom."

"Sometimes," Charlotte Lansing said, with unmistakable ambivalence.

Margo and Alan turned simultaneously to join our conversation, but it was time to leave for the party. We finished our drinks. As I was getting up, Charlotte leaned forward and said:

"I'm so pleased you'll be with us."

five

The four of us walked together up Fifth Avenue. The snowfall was heavier; buildings vanished into a bright opacity. I walked beside Charlotte, making small talk.

"Have you been to the zoo?" I asked. It was just ahead in the park.

"No, I haven't," she said. "Anyway, zoos depress me. The creatures are prisoners."

"Do you identify with them?"

She turned, meeting my eyes. "Yes," she said. "What about you?"

I smiled.

"Do you envy anyone?" she asked.

I thought for a moment. "No," I said.

"That's pride speaking. Most relationships begin with envy. It's the soul of curiosity."

"You think?"

"Not the corrosive kind, envy as wonder about what it would be like to be in someone else's shoes, someone else's circumstances."

"Women envy other women."

"And men envy other men. It's the foundation of many relationships. Think about it."

"I suppose that's true. But what do men envy about women, and vice versa?"

"Everything they don't know about the opposite sex."

I looked at her finely chiseled profile, green eyes, and platinum blond hair with, I had to admit, some wonder. "What's it like for you to walk into a room?"

She smiled at the flattery.

"I mean it. How do you keep men from throwing themselves at you?"

She looked at me again. "Sometimes that's what I want."

That comment earned a moment of silence.

Alan and Margo were ten paces ahead. We crossed Fifth Avenue together, spreading into a loose formation, resuming our tandem arrangement on the other side.

"Am I being too forward?" she said.

"Should I believe you're being forward at all?"

"We seem to be at the same level of despair." She spoke in a laughing tone.

Her candor was disarming. "Is it that obvious?"

She moved close to me and whispered, "Jason, would you like to fuck me tonight at the party?"

"I think I would, yes," I said, shocked, charmed, "if we can manage it." I was suddenly and cravenly under a spell of beauty and desire.

"We'll manage it; leave it to me. It will make the evening more enjoyable."

"I don't doubt that."

We approached the brownstone. As I guided Charlotte up the steps behind Margo and Alan, I was thinking how physical beauty blinds men to problems women have. It's a brave stroke to make a bold proposition, and I admired Charlotte's nerve, but I wondered what volume of discontent fuels renegade sexual brio.

Cynthia Meeker welcomed us warmly; she and her husband were the sort of happy couple that make marriage seem natural and effortless. The house was decorated for New Year's Eve with holly and lights and candles; there was a fire in the fireplace. I'm not a fan of large cocktail parties; I tend to have the same conversation over and over and at the end of the evening I can't remember a thing about anyone. Margo knew quite a few guests professionally and it was easy to see that everybody seemed to be having a good time. I stood by the bookshelves flanking the fireplace, imagining Charlotte in different erotic configurations. I was content in this but soon felt conspicuously solitary and abstracted and so drifted back into the mix.

Eventually Charlotte and I were face-to-face. "Are you enjoying yourself?" she said, a social smile satirically fixed on her expression.

"I'm entertaining fantasies."

"I found a place you might like to see."

"Really?"

"A library upstairs. Meet me there in ten minutes."

I nodded, and she walked off. A woman in a green dress sidled up to me; we introduced ourselves and chatted insipidly for a few minutes until others joined us, making a small circle that allowed me to disengage into other social cells that formed and dissipated in the room; eventually I drifted to the stairway.

Upstairs, Charlotte gestured from a doorway down the hall.

The library was small but cozy, with a couch, a leather Biarritz chair, and wooden-shuttered windows. I closed the door; we fell into a tight embrace and kissed with the keen pleasure of forbidden lust.

"You like the danger, don't you?" she whispered.

I smiled. "You like to take chances."

She was urgent. She pulled at my belt; I tore off her jacket, unbuttoned her blouse, unhooked her bra at the front. Her large breasts fell into my hands, into my mouth. "My husband would kill you if knew we were here like this."

"Dying for this seems a small thing." Her green eyes flashed: I saw a little girl with something like gratitude in her aspect.

On the couch we could see ourselves in the mirror. She lay back and watched animal lust glaze my eyes: I stare into a cunt to find God. I turned her around so that she was kneeling and we watched our reflection in the mirror; my hand rested on the crown of her head in a kind of priestly benediction as I moved up and over her, into her; then nothing mattered in the world but this pleasure out of reach of reason. "Pull my hair," she said. *"Pull my hair!"* I ripped the pin from her bun and seized her braid, pulling it hard to make her head go back and expose her throat; her eyes watched mine sideways from how I held her and she could see these erotic degradations igniting darker fantasies in me. And that's what she wanted: she was a decadent princess and I was the mad monk; she was the debutante and I was her best friend's father; she was the girl next door, the beauty queen, the sad-eyed lady wandering deliriously to whom I had offered help and comfort and then betrayed; she was the mother, wife, daughter of my neighbor; she was my first fuck with Madeline; *she was Alan Lansing's wife following my commands to do this, and then that,* until whatever I was for her found its flash as something we experienced together, exploding in a million-visaged pleasure, her eyes searching mine, her

spirit flown out of her in spasms of wonder, annihilation, disbelief. . . .

The Acela train was pulling into Penn Station; I felt a heaviness of
heart. It was time to start thinking of Margo and Paris. I was not
charmed to learn of her affair; she was not pleased about my
move to St. Croix. Too much had been put off for too long, and
it was clear that a breaking point had been reached. Yet why
should I fault Margo for an affair when it came on the heels of
mine with Charlotte, which went on for months?

As we slowed, I stood and reached for my bag. The mother in
front of me was still barking at her child, who was still whining.
Mercifully, the cell phone man was silent. The other one with
the magazines had put them away, but people like him have a
gift for broadcasting their futility. Now he was stabbing his Palm
Pilot with a stylus like the last sailor on a sinking ship firing off a
final SOS.

six

After the party I tried to forget Charlotte Lansing. I didn't call her; I didn't talk about her to anyone; it was just one of those things, I told myself. I didn't want it to mean anything. I was doing pretty well with it until the first week in February, when I was working at home and the phone rang.

"Hi. It's Charlotte."

"Hi."

"I want to see you. Is that all right?"

We met at a place called the Abbey Pub on West 105th Street near Broadway, a restaurant small enough and dark enough and far enough uptown to be discreet. I was sitting on the other end of the bar. In mid-afternoon it was empty. She came in wearing an exquisitely tailored leather coat. Silhouetted by the light, she made me think of Chopin's sultry B-flat waltz. I took her by the hand and led her into the dining room. We sat in the corner.

"I didn't want to see you again," she said.

"I didn't want to see you, either."

"Are you sorry I called?"

"Do I seem sorry?"

She smiled, looked down, and began to fidget with her ring. Then she took my hand and squeezed it. A current went through me. "I feel like the worst slut."

"Don't be silly."

"I can't keep my hands off myself thinking about that night."

She took my hand and put it between her legs. She had nothing on under the coat, not a stitch. Her eyes had the tense glee of a teenage girl in heat. I put my mouth to her ear. "You *are* a slut," I whispered.

"I told you."

She unbuttoned the bottom of the coat and put my fingers where her legs had spread; her orgasm began almost immediately; when she finished she took a deep breath.

"I had to see you. I know it's crazy; it's just my unhappiness, but this feels so good, you and me."

"I feel the same way," I told her. "But I've tried to put it off."

"Don't put it off. I want you to believe in it." She took my hand and squeezed it tightly. I was thinking how beauty and money and sex all at once are dangerous.

Sometimes a woman appears out of nowhere and you feel irresistible attraction and you realize it's the same for her and you also realize that you're in the grip of an impossible situation. I couldn't see any upside to an affair with Charlotte. She was married to a successful and powerful man. They had a rich life. My marriage was unstable and an affair was a symptom of things I didn't want to face about my situation. Why should

I get involved with her? It wasn't smart in a million ways. Her eyes were reading my mind.

"Let's get a room," I said.

She grabbed her bag. I paid the check and we left.

seven

When I retired from the dot-com world I frequently went flying the way others go sailing or play golf. My favorite day trip was low along the beaches of Long Island Sound, past Newport, Rhode Island, out to Edgartown on Martha's Vineyard. There is a large grass airfield near town on the south shore called Katama. Besides an airfield, it's a wildlife preserve, where fragrant wild roses and Queen Anne's lace grow among the thick briars that border the runways. On any given summer day pilots from as far away as two hundred miles fly in to spend a pleasant few hours there; familiar faces and familiar planes abound. My friend Mike Creato manages the airport; he grew up there and in the warm months gives thrill rides in his 1941 red Waco biplane.

On one of those rare summer days when the light is golden and the air still, I landed and parked my Beech 18 by the white fence at Whosie's, the restaurant there, and walked over to

Mike's hangar to say hello. The cowling was off his biplane; he was working on his engine.

"What's up?"

"Changing a sparkle plug."

A minute passed with no further talk between us, this interval in accordance with the willfully slower pace there; I stood in the sun watching Mike put the wrench to his motor. It's peaceful at Katama; you can smell the ocean mingled with the sweet scent of berries and honeysuckle that grow in the brambles.

"I heard about a job you might want to consider," Mike said, peering at a cluster of wires.

"Not interested. I've discovered there are few pleasures more pure than watching someone else at work."

"Ever hear of the Grumman Albatross?" he said.

"The big flying boat?"

"Right. A twin-engine amphibian. You'd like it."

"I might."

"There's a guy in Florida flying them."

"Where?"

"Out of Miami."

"What's the operation called?"

"Island Airboats. He runs charters. It's a kind of nostalgia idea. The fun part is flying the HU-16 Albatross, the biggest amphibian Grumman built, the one designed for open ocean search and rescue."

"How many does he operate?"

He's got two in Miami, on Watson Island, but he wants to set up a base on St. Croix, maybe get a third."

Mike knew what was happening in a certain stratum of aviation the way some people know about minor-league baseball.

"How many passengers can it hold?"

"In the airline configuration it can carry thirty-three in the back, but he's got most of the seats out. The cabin is done like a yacht in mahogany veneer. I've seen pictures; it's beautiful. He uses the ramps from Charlie Blair's old operation."

"Antilles Air Boats?"

"He's bringing the flying boat back to the Caribbean."

I knew the Albatross and respected its beauty and function. There are some objects made by human hands that combine art and utility in near-perfect balance, where competing considerations of design intersect at the object's truth, so to speak. The Albatross was an airplane, but it was also a sixty-foot yacht, with a seven-plus-foot beam and a ninety-six-foot wingspan impressive to behold. It had truth; anyone could see that right away; it had the high dignity of a schooner under full sail, and something of the majesty of, say, the *Queen Mary*.

"He may have a good idea," Mike said. "People seem to like classic machines."

"You make a living with a biplane, so you would know. What's his name?"

"Jack Hibbard. Call him."

"So you think this Jack Hibbard is looking for pilots?"

"I know he is. But he's looking for a particular kind of pilot." Mike threw a glance at the Beech 18.

"What about you?" I said.

"I'm too busy with the business here, and I've got the sailboat in Fort Lauderdale when the season's finished. We migrate in November. Rebecca likes the boat; she looks forward to it. She'd get mad if I took a job in winter."

"How is Rebecca?"

"We're getting married."

"Really!"

"She likes it here on the island and goes with the flow. We're having a good time."

Mike is one of those rare individuals who are purely and unapologetically themselves. Rebecca's like that, too. She took a thrill ride one afternoon and moved in with Mike a week later. It must have been some thrill. They've been together ever since.

He opened a drawer on the red toolbox and pulled out another ratchet. He worked the ratchet until he extracted the spark plug he had been unscrewing and held it up, examining it as if it were a sacred artifact. Then he pointed it at me.

"I can see you in a flying boat, Jason; I really can. You ought to look into it." Now he was being serious. He knew I needed to fly an airplane with a pulse and a heartbeat; he also knew I was giving thought to a job of some sort in aviation, and he knew my domestic situation was tenuous. "Give it a shot, what the hell."

"I may just do that."

Mike got my imagination running. I called Miami that very afternoon and spoke to Jack Hibbard. He was friendly on the phone. He told me to come down and have a look at the operation and we'd talk. Suddenly, living in the Caribbean as a pilot was an idea with a lot of appeal. A complete break with all things familiar combining tropical islands and flying was not the worst idea to consider under the circumstances.

eight

The following week I flew the Twin Beech down to Opa Locka Airport and took a taxicab to the pad on Watson Island where two Albatross flying boats were parked under palm trees beside the inland waterway. One of them happened to be starting its engines. I stood off to the side and watched the motors come to life, blowing great clouds of blue smoke at first. The pilots ran through their checks, and when the big ship began to move, the Captain waved as he went by.

I watched it go down the ramp into the water, feeling something like the excitement of my first sight of an airplane up close. I had a fair amount of diverse flying experience, but the Albatross was unique. Once it was afloat, the pilot retracted the landing gear and the wheels went up into the fuselage. The Albatross navigated slowly and majestically down the channel until it got to the waterway. There it turned to the south, and when the power came up a great spray made it disappear.

The noise of the propellers was deafening. As it gathered speed it rose out of the spray like a breaching whale, going faster until it moved like a speedboat, the spray clean and even behind it. When it lifted into the air and banked gently eastward toward the white and pink clouds out to sea, I thought how now as a graceful flying ship it was twice or three times in grandeur what the boat had been.

The Florida sun was bright on the white concrete. The grass was thick and short and very green against the base of the operations shack. The shack was made from cinder block and painted bright yellow. The smell of sea salt and the tilt of palm trees in the early heat, with the airboats and the ships in the harbor, made a strong impression.

"Think you'd like to try that?"

I turned to the voice behind me; Jack Hibbard was standing in the doorway of the operations shack.

"Yes, I would," I said. "I'm Jason Walker." We shook hands.

"Come on in."

Inside, it was cool. There were pictures of flying boats and fishing boats and other airplanes on the walls of his office. The walls were also yellow and the windows were green, with wooden venetian blinds to keep down the light and heat of afternoon. A bookcase held mostly logbooks and technical manuals in binders, some histories of early airlines, and a volume of federal aviation regulations. It was a comfortable space.

Jack was the owner and chief pilot. A few years older than I, probably forty-five, he was taller than average, with a full head of dark, somewhat curly hair and round blue eyes that seemed more sensitive than the rougher-looking rest of him. He had big callused hands and wore the generic flying clothes of 1947 or now: blue ball cap, dark slacks, and a colored short-sleeve shirt.

In fact, everything here had a timeless feel to it, something Jack could see I appreciated.

"Have a seat. Make yourself comfortable." Jack sat behind his desk, which I noticed was uncluttered and neatly organized.

"Ever fly seaplanes?"

"Small single-engine floatplanes once, just to get the rating."

"It's a little different in the flying boat."

"I'm sure it is." I laughed.

"Tell me about your background." Jack sat back and folded his hands on his stomach with the comfort of a king in a counting-house.

I told him the basic facts of my life. I had grown up in the Northeast, in a town not far from New York City, and had learned to fly at a nearby airport during high school.

"I have an aunt, my father's stepsister, named Madeline Singer, who flew the air-show circuit in the seventies."

"What did she fly?"

"Pitts Special."

Jack thought for a second. "I've met her. At Oshkosh. Very attractive, as I recall, and she put on a great show. She was married to Tom Phillips."

"That's Madeline. She took me flying when I was ten years old and I just assumed everyone who flew airplanes turned them upside down and inside out. I couldn't wait to get my license."

I told Jack I'd been a flight instructor in college, and had flown jumpers, and had done some crop dusting in Alabama during one summer before joining the Air Force Reserves. Crop dusting piqued his interest.

"What were you dusting for?"

"Fire ants, mostly."

"What'd you fly?"

"Ag Cats and Pawnees."

"That Ag Cat's a good machine."

"Yes, it is."

The Cat was a Grumman product and so from the same family as the Albatross.

"Do you have much round-engine time?"

"I own a Beech 18. I just flew it down from New York."

His eyebrows went up and he leaned forward. "You have it with you?"

"Over at Opa Locka."

He leaned back again, smiling broadly. "I've got a couple of thousand hours in the Beech 18."

"So you've had some good times."

Jack nodded. "A few. I was up in Alaska with it for a couple of years, flying the North Slope."

"No kidding," I said. "I was up in Alaska last year, at Emerald Lake, about an hour east of Anchorage."

Jack knew the lake. "Do you know Terry Smith? He and his wife operate a turbine Goose out of Anchorage, Aleutian Goose Adventures."

I'd met them.

Aviation is a brotherhood of unscribed castes, and pilots communicate in a language like horse breeders. The Grumman amphibians, the Ag Cat, and the Twin Beech mattered to Jack. He knew the skill it took to fly these airplanes. The Ag Cat was a biplane, built sturdy for rough flying. It had round engines similar to the Albatross and the Twin Beech. The technical difference between a round engine and a modern one is not great, except in the relationship the pilot must establish with it. If flying is an art based on a science, there is more art to understanding the character of a round engine. Those who operate them appreciate this. A round engine speaks to you, but you have to have ears that listen to what it's saying. It was clear to me that mastering the Albatross would require a combination of special sensitivities that cannot be taught or learned. Jack was mainly concerned that I had those sensitivities, and I could see he was satisfied that I did.

"I'm thinking of basing one of the planes on St. Croix. Could you see yourself living there?"

"I'd like to try it."

"Plan on that, then. When can you come to work?"

"Tomorrow."

He laughed. This pleased him.

"I'll have to go back to New York soon and settle affairs," I told him, "but I can stay for the week and we can begin to train."

"Works for me," Jack Hibbard said. We shook hands across the desk. We would have no problem getting along.

He pulled two blue binders from the bookshelf behind him. "These are your operating manuals. Meet me here at eight to-morrow morning. We'll begin ground school. It's pretty infor-mal. We'll climb into one of the planes and I'll point out the switches and tell you what they do; we'll talk about water oper-ations; then we'll go flying."

"Sounds good."

He walked me to the door and we shook hands again. "Wel-come aboard," he said.

Mike Creato had been right. This operation seemed to suit me. Once qualified, I'd be flying over some of the most beauti-ful beaches in the world, a far cry from cellular telephones and computer screens. I stood on the ramp outside while I waited for the taxi to my hotel. The remaining Albatross sat silently in the shadows of palm trees while behind it the mast of a sailboat glided improbably along the rooflines of homes on the water-way. This was a different world. Later, I was amazed at how swiftly and dramatically life can change.

part two

For we do not know the whereabouts of what we are seeking . . .

—M. Proust

nine

Charlotte and I saw each other twice a month from February through June. The Abbey Pub became our meeting place. Sometimes we went to a hotel, sometimes to the apartment of a friend of hers on the East Side. The apartment was spacious and bright and reminded me of my aunt Madeline's place on Park Avenue, warm in my memory for similar reasons.

"Does Alan know about us?"

"I don't think so. Why?"

"Did you know he screwed me out of a land deal?"

"Tell me about it."

Alan Lansing was a venture capitalist with a dubious reputation, a real Gordon Gecko, a man with an inflated sense of himself and contempt for other people. I had discovered an island for sale on Moosehead Lake, in Maine. The house on it had been empty for several years. The owner died with no immediate relatives, and his heirs wanted a fast sale to pay taxes on other properties. The price was low.

I found out about it through a friend who lived in Bangor and knew the executor. I asked him to send me photos. The house, formerly a lodge, stood in roughly the geographic center of a twenty-acre island. There were two boat landings with wooden docks and a concrete ramp; dirt paths led to the main house through the woods. It was a beautiful place that needed work, but emotional healing welcomes that sort of challenge; in time it would make a fine camp, as the cabins and more spectacular homes in that region are called. When I told Margo, she got excited about it, too, and part of it was a sense that our marriage might heal in such a wholesome natural environment. It was not to happen.

We were attending one of those charity dinners that mark certain professions for compulsory attendance. Alan and Charlotte were there, the first time I had seen them as a couple since New Year's Eve. For the most part we ignored each other. Making small talk before dinner, I happened to mention the Maine property to friends. Alan overheard me. The next morning he bought it out from under us with cash. I was furious. I called his office.

"I don't know what you're saying," he said, dissembling.

"Let me help you to understand," I said, drumming a pencil in rapid ruffles. "You overheard me talking about that property and went behind my back."

"There's a rule of life and business, I suppose," he said, in the droll tone of a man examining his cuticles. "First come, first served."

There was no talking to him. Double-dealing gave him a thrill; he loved to spoil; he lived to gloat. But I'm not a person who forgets or forgives. The camp in Maine was another try at believing in a future with Margo; losing it burst that bubble, so in some sense Alan Lansing played a part in the timing of our divorce. But that was a small dose, and I may be carping.

"I hate him," Charlotte said.

A more serious encounter with his sociopathic ethics happened six months later, during the sale of one of the dot-coms I brought out. Alan contrived a greenmail threat that cost my principals millions and nearly cut me out of a portion of my stock.

I had been a marketing executive in print media. Three young, smart, computer-savvy scientists came to me through a headhunter. They had developed a more advanced search engine for the Internet and wanted me to sell it. They were way ahead of their time. No one was yet sure how revenue could be most effectively generated; no specific marketing strategies had evolved. In a real sense we were pioneers; our success was the product of creative trial and error. After coming on board I developed new advertising instruments, some of which were abandoned, some of which exist today; we found subscribers by the hundreds, then by the thousands, and the profits started rolling in.

Alan Lansing's specialty was finding companies in a vulnerable state, either on the way up or on the way down. He was like a predator attacking only the old or the young in a herd. He'd identify a target, then raise enough capital to get controlling interest. Once in control, he'd advertise a new business plan while he sold the company piecemeal until it was a shell. When there was nothing left of any value, the shell was kept afloat with money from pension funds on a promise of a future. When that was gone, and after he paid himself and his colleagues a rich bonus, the company would be liquidated and he'd move on to the next target. He did this over and over, generating millions in unearned income.

When my company began to find real success we became vulnerable to a takeover. Wall Street was watching. When the word got out that we were seeking a merger, Alan Lansing and his crew began circling above the offers that started coming our way. There was one company especially well matched for us, and we wanted to make a deal. All seemed to be going smoothly when suddenly negotiations cooled. We learned that Alan Lansing's group had moved on that company in a takeover initiative. It was a greenmail ploy; we were the real target. When my principals voted a compromise Alan Lansing's group backed off, allowing them to broker our deal for a fat commission, a fee of several million that amounted to extortion. It was a lesson in vulture capitalism. I quickly put it behind me, but memory is long and life has a strange way of settling scores, as I've learned.

"He must know about us," Charlotte acknowledged. "He'll continue to come at you."

Charlotte's beauty was hypnotic, but something desperate about her worried me, and her husband had insinuated himself into my affairs; I didn't like it. The idea of being followed was too much; Charlotte was feeling it, too. The relationship was tangled and had nowhere to go; it seemed obvious to both of us it had to end, and the reality of it finally broke through.

"I don't think we should see each other anymore," she said.

"Are you sure?"

"You don't need an angry husband interfering with your life. That's what's been happening; I'm certain of it."

Gloomy but also relieved, we spent the rest of the afternoon in a pagan passion, believing it was the last time.

Leaving a love affair is a gradual process, like grieving, and you're never sure how much of spirit was spent. Nothing seems changed at first. Then the pain begins; emptiness feeds on memories for a while until the soul you gave away returns to its solitary place in the heart. Later it may seem like folly, or unfold as something much larger than merely passion; once touched, emotions are altered in ways not always apparent. I withdrew into a ruminative state culminating in the flight to Alaska and the certainty that changes were necessary if my life had any possibility of meaning something beyond growing symptoms of frustration.

ten

My usual rule of thumb with a new airplane is that it takes a hundred hours to really get to know it. You establish the relationship hour by hour, feeling the contours of performance, how the ship responds at different speeds, learning what to do and when to do it so that the beast doesn't turn on you. By a hundred hours you should have an understanding. For every other airplane I've flown this has been the case. This is not true of the Albatross amphibious flying boat. The variables of water and wind are infinite. Tides, currents, crosswinds, waves, swells, narrow channels, sudden storms, and other vessels create an ever-changing scope of challenges. No two days are alike; no two hours are alike; conditions can vary from minute to minute. You have to read the wind on the water, and the water itself, then pick your place of landing to allow for safe taxi back to the ramp. The Albatross is a large ship without a rudder; the

Captain uses differential power and reverse thrust to maneuver. When twenty-seven thousand pounds of mass change course in a sudden gust of wind, quick work is all that will save it from bad result. Now add an engine failure into the mix. So this is an art that requires many more than a hundred hours to master.

I spent the first morning sitting in the cockpit making myself familiar with the layout as Jack talked me through the systems.

"The throttles are overhead," he said. "The propellers are controlled with these electric switches."

He showed me how the fuel transfer system worked, moving fuel from the float tanks to the main tanks. The Albatross carries enough fuel for ten hours of flight. He showed me the hydraulic system and the emergency hand pump to lower or raise the landing gear in the event of main pump failure. He showed me the bow compartment where the anchors and lines were stowed, and the cargo bins in the watertight compartments under the cabin floor. There was a lavatory behind the aft bulkhead, a shower for the crew, and hammocks that could be slung on fixtures in the cabin or strung between the landing gear and the wing when there were lazy hours with nothing to do.

By noontime it was too hot to stay in the airplane. Jack left me to my own resources and went back to the operations shack to work. I took the manuals to a picnic table under the palm trees and studied them. It wasn't a complicated airplane, just a big one; it required two pilots, a Captain and a First Officer. I'd start out flying from the right seat, and after a journeymanship where I learned the ins and outs of the aircraft and its operation I'd move up to Captain. After lunch, Jack took me for my first flight.

"We'll just take her up and do a few landings on the water to give you the idea."

I read the checklist, and his hand moved swiftly through the array of switches and levers.

"Hydraulic bypass."

"Checked."

"Unfeather/unreverse switches."

"Checked."

"Prop oil replenishing switches."

"Checked and guarded."

"Gang bar switches."

"Up and off."

"Starting the right engine."

I pressed the starter button and the prop began to turn. Jack counted six blades, checking for hydraulic lock. "Now tickle the primer as I throw the switches," he said. I pressed and released the primer button just above the starter in quick succession and the engine easily came to life. After both engines were up to temperature and running smoothly we ran the safety checks, testing the magnetos and the propellers. When those checks were finished we were set to go.

"Ready?"

I nodded. "Clear on the right."

Both engines running, Jack advanced the throttles and the plane began to move out from under the palm trees toward the water. He approached the ramp slowly. The angle seemed steep as we went down; the nose went in the water farther and farther until we became buoyant and I could feel the wheels lift off the concrete. Now we were a boat; Jack let us drift into the channel. He held his hand up, palm down, moving it back and forth for emphasis. "Always keep looking for traffic. Speedboats, Jet Skis, they come out of nowhere and surprise you."

We followed the channel in the same manner as the ship I had seen the day before. Our eyes swept the area ahead. When we turned south on the wider water Jack said, "Ready for take-off?" I nodded. He moved the throttles slowly forward and the engines began to whine and the propellers were very loud. I watched Jack handle the control wheel: he held it back and made large aileron inputs at the slower speeds, and ever smaller inputs as acceleration made the flight control surfaces effective. Liftoff from the water had that special exhilaration of all graceful vessels in their performing element. The Albatross banked gently, a large, imposing plane.

We flew north to Lake Okeechobee to practice, where I watched Jack perform near-impossible maneuvers with panache. He landed so smoothly I didn't know when we touched down. He could make the big boat turn circles on the water; he could taxi into tight corners and back it onto beaches.

"You take it," he said. I took the control wheel in my right hand and put my left hand on the throttles above the center console. There is a tendency to overcontrol with power. "Pick a point on the horizon and steer for it. Use your flight controls to help sail. Stay slow on the water while you taxi, and keep your eyes moving."

More easily said than done. Massive and rudderless, the airboat had a mind of its own in my hands. It moved left and right in exaggerated gyrations.

"You're overcorrecting," Jack said. "Make small power changes."

I began to feel the plane. By attenuating the throttle movements and following through with flight control inputs made the ship begin to sail a straight course.

"Now try reverse thrust. Slow us down to a standstill and maintain the heading. Remember, you have about a four-second lag at idle between the time you go into reverse and when reverse thrust becomes effective. Take that into consideration and you'll have better control."

He was right. You had to think in a broader time frame. "Keep the control wheel back. And consider the wind. That's the important thing. Which direction is it coming from?"

We practiced for a couple of hours and did many takeoffs and landings. Landing the Albatross was a special thrill; it settled onto the water smoothly, like a great swan. Flying it, to borrow Graham Greene's response to his initial experience with opium, "was like the first sight of a beautiful woman with whom one realizes a relationship is possible."

eleven

The following week I was sitting in the right seat enjoying my first flight through the Bahamas as an airboat pilot. Our passengers were a young couple and their daughter. We also carried some freight. The little girl kept her face pressed to the window, calling her mother's attention to beaches and boats we passed over.

The Albatross allowed a view of earth more fascinating than the sterile distractions modern airliners offer. We were never on instruments, always visual and low. We passed south of Nassau, and I could see a long chain of islands extending to the horizon.

"Those are the Exumas," Jack said. "Take a look at those beaches; sometimes we land down there. You have to be careful. Where the channels are narrow the current is swift."

We banked over the bow of a private yacht. Naked sun worshipers lying on towels waved enthusiastically. The islands stretched out before us as far as the eye could see. The waters were deep blue until they got shallow; then they were green. You could see yellow sandbars sculpted by currents; great black shadows ran on the sea's surface under low drifting clouds.

"That's Staniel Cay. See the airstrip?"

I nodded. Beneath us passed a three-thousand-foot asphalt runway near a small harbor village. There were stilt cabins, and great yachts, and lighthouses and small coves with sailboats; there were monuments and prisons; there were graveyards and churches with steeples and many secret places of beauty visible from the air. The engines ran smoothly, and the propellers ran smoothly as we flew low over long white beaches with five-story dunes and other boats and tiny villages in the sun. In these vast stretches of virgin sands there were only occasional persons walking; when they waved it gave you a strong sense that if you had a day of life left you'd want to live it this way.

"I never get tired of this," Jack said, and I knew what he meant: life as a dream was the pure experience of flight, and we were having it.

Six hours after we departed from Miami, the hills of St. Thomas appeared on the horizon. Jack swept into a left turn as we made our approach to the harbor; the hull touched down like a giant water ski, skidding on the waves. We slowed quickly and made for the downtown ramp. Once we were on land, ground crews approached with stairs for our three passengers; then the crew began to unload the cargo while Jack and I strolled along the docks. I was exhilarated.

An hour later I was starting the engines for the short flight to St. Croix. I taxied to the ramp, and as we floated off the concrete again I felt how the Albatross became a different creature altogether on the unresisting water.

Jack continued to coach me. "Try playing with the power."

There was no traffic ahead in the harbor, so I moved the right throttle up and the plane turned to the left, then I moved the left throttle up and it turned to the right.

"Try reverse."

I brought both throttles back to idle and pushed up on them with the heel of my hand. They clicked over a stop and I could hear the sound of the propellers change pitch as they pushed the air forward, slowing the Albatross.

"Ready for takeoff?" I said, turning into the wind.

"Let's go."

I held the control wheel back and pushed the throttles up slowly. At full power the nickel-plated propellers were roaring, sucking water back as a dense spray. I held the control wheel firmly back to get the bow up. At thirty knots I relaxed back pressure and the bow moved forward onto the step and the hull accelerated to flying speed. At sixty-five knots I eased back on the control wheel and we broke the water's surface and were airborne. I turned gently southbound toward St. Croix, visible in the blue distance.

Some airplanes have an aura, a Zen about them, like certain ships or buildings do. The Albatross exerted an influence on those who would fly it, insisting on a level of excellence equal to its own considerable virtues. I sensed there was much to learn where airmanship met seamanship. I knew to take nothing for granted. I could see it was not a plane that you fought in the air or on the water, but one you had to work with on its own terms. An airplane will humble false pride, and an Albatross would accomplish that faster than most. It had truth and it gave truth to those who flew it.

"I love this kind of flying," I told Jack. I was exuberant.

He laughed. "So you're pretty sure you want to continue?" Jack wanted to be sure I understood the marginal aspects of the job.

"I'm not in it for the money," I said.

"St. Croix has had some problems, but it's improving. Tax incentives have brought new business down. There are some staunch part-time residents, and the tourist trade is coming back. The native population is more receptive than it once was, so I think we've got a good chance here."

"I'm in," I said.

But even as I embraced this new existence I knew I had a lot of personal housekeeping to attend to. "I need a few weeks to go back and sort things out," I told him. "There are some marriage issues."

"Take all the time you need. I'm working out the local approvals for establishing a base here. That'll take a month at least. Go back and take care of whatever you need to, and then plan to be down here in late October."

"I appreciate it."

"Not a problem," he said.

We spent the rest of the evening at Stixx, a restaurant and bar on the boardwalk. The harbor was calm and very pretty under moonlight. In the morning we returned to Miami.

After the trip, Jack drove me to Miami International, where all the flights to New York were full. A helpful agent suggested I fly to Boston instead and connect with the Acela to New York. "You'll only lose a few hours if you live in the city." She was right, although I wasn't in a hurry.

Margo and I had planned a vacation to France earlier in the year and decided to go ahead with our travel plans. We both found relief in the thought of Paris as a buffer for bad blood; absorbed into its art and architecture we could be intimate at arm's length and broach uncomfortable subjects without suffocating. This wasn't explicitly verbalized but rather expressed in overaffirmative accord that struck a false note.

twelve

I stood on the Pont Neuf and saw the Paris of my imagination, a city of monuments and cathedrals and magnificent hotels, where (so I imagined) writing and art still mattered, and where lovers and friends talked into the night at sidewalk cafés on leafy boulevards.

Later, we sat in the warm early-evening air drinking our wine silently, waiting for our meal. Giant clouds drifted above us like strange uncommanded vessels. Trees rustled softly in a gentle wind, and late sunlight made leaves shine like silver. Shadows fell across the sidewalk in a complicated geometry. There were no words. There were no feelings, except anxiety fighting unsuccessfully against that black mood when the world seems inhuman. Like a chanted phrase, Margo's identity began to dissolve in front of me. I looked at her face, with its interesting angular authority, her eyes once so alluring; now she seemed strange to my memories. Our silence amplified the strain between us, or rather it stood for how we had become invisible to each other.

The waiter brought our dinner. I had the duck confit with a crisp skin and small potatoes sliced wafer thin; they seemed to float off the plate. I was about to comment on it, but Margo spoke.

"What's wrong with us?" she said.

"Aren't you having a good time?" I replied.

"It's difficult, that's all." She sighed; then her aspect brightened. "But it's wonderful in ways, really; I've been looking forward to it."

There were many interpretations I could give to what she said, but that, too, was one of our problems. Margo was equivocal, famous for appearing at the last minute to go anywhere. I said to her once, "You're always almost late."

She thought for a moment and fired back, "So what you're saying is I'm always early, because you're either early, on time, or late."

Margo was a lawyer.

Our legal system, like our national conscience, is tortured by equivocations. When language becomes ethereal, meaning is ambiguous, nothing coheres, no one is accountable, and the world is absurd. Our marriage had become like that. Margo was imploring us to be honest with each other, but I understood enough of her complexity to see that she took a certain pleasure in my pain, even if she was feeling it herself.

"This duck is fabulous," I said. "Would you like a taste?"

"Mmm," she muttered, meaning, No. The rest of the evening had that same thematic disinclination to share.

The following afternoon, we were sitting at a café table in St. Germain, at rue Bonaparte across from the church. The sun fell through the trees, making dappled shadows on the sidewalk that looked like so many gold coins.

"I wish it could stay like this," Margo said, almost exuberantly.

"It's a beautiful day," I agreed.

"What I mean is that good moments pass too quickly. Look at us."

She was speaking in code: life was passing her by, and I was the folly that had consumed her youth.

After lunch we went walking—to the BNP at Grenelle to cash some traveler's checks, then to the metro, to station Charles de Gaulle, emerging at the Arc de Triomphe, where we started down the Champs-Elysées, stopping for a glass of wine at a sidewalk table with a view of the wide descending boulevard. It felt thrilling to be in the great city again, and for isolated finite periods of time anything seemed possible.

"Have you ever thought of living in a foreign country?" Margo squinted at the sun. She conspicuously stretched her legs into the sidewalk. Men began to notice them.

"Occasionally," I said.

I felt discouraged to know how attractive she appeared to others and how little able I was to appreciate her myself.

"I feel so at home here," she said.

"We seem to feel at home everywhere—except at home."

She turned her head abruptly and anger flashed in her eyes. "You didn't have to say that." And she was right. It was precisely the sort of comment each was most watchful for and unforgiving of in the other.

We finished our wine, and the noontime bustle began to thin. The heat of early afternoon challenged stamina. "I want to go back to the hotel for a little while," Margo said.

Our hotel was only a block away. We had come to the George V without reservations, but I had stayed there once before and praised it to the desk clerk. The manager happened to be standing nearby and gave us a three-room suite for the regular room rate. This trip was fated with ironies.

The living room looked out across avenue George V. I poured some vodka and sat back to enjoy the view. Travel overstimulates my mind, and I often find it difficult to read after a long walk. Margo had gone into the bathroom. Ten or fifteen minutes passed; I lost track. Her voice brought me out of a reverie. She called me into the bedroom. Our bedroom had a blackout curtain, Margo closed it. A thin splinter of light fell across her face. "Make love to me," she said.

"I can't," I told her.

Her eyes bore into mine. Suddenly I was face-to-face with regions of great loss. Margo wasn't Margo anymore, and I was no longer myself; I was frightened to touch her. I needed light, and air, yearning in the heart, and some life other than the fraud this one had become. By means of a most complicated complicity, we had managed to transform the essence of pleasure into the purest part of pain.

Later, as the metro moved swiftly through its labyrinth beneath the city, the clamor of it grew like an audio hallucination and I was thinking how clinical our sex had become. The thought depressed me profoundly. I was sure Margo felt the same thing.

We had come to Paris hoping to identify our marriage. Relationships that drift apart can drift together again, or so we believed. Maybe I was bored, or maybe depressed; in any case, the marriage seemed hopeless, and if one part of me lobbied to continue, another part was desperate to be free. An emotional disquiet seemed to press on every mood.

We resurfaced at Odeon and walked through narrow streets, past charming sidewalk cafés, to the dome of the Institut de France, and across the pont des Arts to the Louvre. I had a fragile thought about the meaning of the pyramid. I wondered what Margo's impressions were, but I didn't ask.

Inside the Louvre, the sun slanting through windows on the west face illuminated a long corridor packed with masterpieces of painting and sculpture. I was repeating a line from Bertrand Russell to myself: "The thing about literature that makes it so consoling is that its tragedies are in the past, and have the completeness and repose that comes of being beyond the reach of our endeavors." For several hours Margo and I strolled contentedly in that dreamlike state of open spirit, but the emotional impact of art is subliminal, troubling, and exhausting; after a while it overwhelms.

We left the museum and walked toward the Seine.

"Where to next?" Margo said.

The question seemed barbed, only because we had come to that excruciating moment in a relationship when everything said, seen, and done has a multiple meaning that avers to an uncomfortable truth. I realized suddenly that walking in Paris had been a tour of our relationship somehow. This occurred to me at the Eiffel Tower, where we had gone to watch the sun set. Every city has a carnival attraction. The elevator was crowded, so we got off at the first stop. We didn't go to the top because Margo said the wait didn't seem worth the view. Instead we stood at the rails on the second level. I could see the river and Notre Dame and the roads alive with traffic on the riverbank, a population moving through fixtures of nature and culture, lives interwoven into the fabric of the earth and the rhythms of its days. The city seemed indifferent to our sight of it, all the familiar landmarks at a certain mollifying remove, and I sensed how we understand ourselves perversely: towers are made so people can thrill to a view of the world without them in it.

Great beauty lay before me, and all I could feel was a staggering emptiness. I wanted to weep. Sharing is the only human satisfaction that takes us beyond ourselves; otherwise we exist in solitary confinement. This was the end for us, inevitable, palpable, irrevocable, we both knew it, and it was the last thing we could share, but only from a cold-increasing distance of disillusionment.

"I'm going to leave you," Margo said, squinting into the heavenly light of the magic hour. After that she walked away and disappeared into the crowd.

At first I felt relieved, then abandoned. When I went back to the hotel, the concierge said Margo had taken a taxi to the airport. Later, wandering aimlessly, I tried to put my feelings together, to come to some coherent understanding of them. Besides a sickness of heart, I was afraid of being alone.

thirteen

Losing a marriage is a grief of being lost yourself. I woke alone in the dark Paris hotel bedroom. For long minutes I lay in that half-awake state that slowly opens the mind to lucidity. Margo hovered. I surveyed our life together in abbreviated visions, beginning with our first date: a motorboat, the glow of plankton in our wake, stars bright above us, warm summer air, wind on our faces. We landed on an island beach. The moon was dreamy and bright as we walked along the shore. We went exploring. At some distance through the low brush, we saw the light of a fire. A squatter who lived in an Indian tepee was sitting alone. We hailed him from the shadows and he invited us to join him. The tepee was authentic. He showed us its simple design: long posts covered in canvass and painted in colorful geometric forms. Later we built our own fire and Margo reached for my hand. "I could be happy with you in a tepee," she had said. But not, I thought now, more than a decade later, in handsome circumstances on Central Park West.

I got out of bed, started coffee, and ran a bath. The bath was hot, just short of scalding. Outside, the sky was black at daybreak, with thunder rumbling like advancing war. I was still in the bath when the phone rang.

"It's me." Margo sounded exhausted.

"Where are you?" I was standing by the bed dripping wet, wondering if it was wise to hold a phone to my ear.

"I've just landed in New York and I'm feeling shitty. I was wrong to leave. I'm sorry."

"Obviously we've got some talking to do."

"I shouldn't have run off like that."

"I'm all right. Go home and get some rest."

"Thanks for not being a bastard about it. I really do feel awful."

"Forget it."

We still cared for each other, but the shared illusion was gone, and with it the joy of being together. I appreciated the call. It was her way of confirming the truth of things. I went back to the bath, shivering. The water had grown tepid, so I gave it up and showered instead.

Downstairs a short time later, tourists worried by the weather were standing around restlessly in the lobby, waiting for transportation. I told the desk clerk to thank the manager for the suite, paid the bill, and went outside to get another coffee, stepping around a pile of suitcases and trunks.

On the Champs-Elysées, the clouds were low above the buildings and darkness made people visible inside their offices. You could smell the rain, but it wouldn't fall. People walked in quick steps, glancing up as they went, expecting a downpour at any instant. I hailed a cab and in minutes was on the highway from Paris to CDG.

Then it began to rain hard, bringing traffic to a crawl. Car lights shone through a veil of downpour and the wiper blades beat fast, like something mechanical gone mad. I directed the driver to American Airlines. The B777 jumbos were lined up like steamships and had that nobility of great vessels in port. I have always thrilled to the beginning of a journey, when the spirit whispers all things are possible.

After takeoff I fell asleep almost immediately. When I woke, I peered out and saw Newfoundland beneath the wing in clear air. The land there is stark but beautiful: there are broad beaches, cliffs, hills, rivers and lakes, and country roads that follow the shoreline to tiny villages. I saw two sailboats at anchor in a cove on an island not far from the mainland; the sun was low enough to make them shine brilliantly. The beaches were spare and empty of people, cold beauty with a chilling grandeur that spoke to my uncertain mood. I spent the rest of the flight writing a letter to Margo.

fourteen

Dear Margo,

I've been trying to find a way to articulate to myself, and to you, the feelings and reasons behind our breakup. You told me that this was not something you wanted, and I believe you. It's not something I wanted, either, but it's something that's been on the horizon for a long time, a failure that we resisted and were hoping to avoid.

We had issues, certainly: the fear of boredom and boredom itself; some casual infidelities—I've known about yours and you've suspected mine—apprehensions about the future. Other marriages have survived worse.

In the beginning, we did seem to share our lives happily, but over time, I felt you stop responding to me as who I am; rather it seemed a response to something else, a fear perhaps that had grown up inside, or the ghost of a fear.

How do you approach what isn't there? I tried to express it to you in ways you frequently found insulting. What I meant to say was that a gap between us had grown painfully wide; we weren't sharing average intimacies; you disappeared into your work and I flew off trying to find the next phase. I know you'll say I was escaping from you. Maybe the truth is somewhere in between, where it usually lies.

Relationships are fragile. We take so much for granted as a matter of course, and maybe we shouldn't. We see what we want to see, and ignore what's painful or destructive until we're overrun by it. We have to imagine the best in the individuals we want to have close to us, Margo. We have to respond to the best because the worst is easy to see in anyone. It's easy to find fault and assign blame. If you want somebody in your life, you have to treat them with the kind of respect and admiration perhaps they don't always deserve. We lost sight of that somehow. I know you're a good person, a thoughtful and accomplished woman. And I know that at my worst I'm far from evil; selfish, perhaps, sometimes absurd, but not nasty, never venomous, and, frankly, far less selfish than I pretend to be.

In many ways it would be easier for both of us if the issue was another person. At least the failure of the marriage would not feel so elusive to explanation. But it isn't that. The basic truth is that we (or I, if you wish) have not been up to the task. Other people seem to find a stable sort of happiness, or at least a tolerable togetherness to keep loneliness at bay. The differences between us became too great; maybe it's that simple. Neither of us wants to live a lie and I don't want to be a cause for the sorrow of someone else; life is too short for that, and I get no pleasure from it. We'll work out something amicable and get on with life.

Love,
Jason

The process of divorce is like waking up each morning with somebody else's mental illness. I was sitting with Margo in our living room, enjoying the familiar view of Central Park. She was smoking again: an impulse to find me complicit in this hovered briefly and then passed; she raised her eyebrows to express disgust, exhaled resignedly while staring at the coal, then stabbed out the cigarette violently. She looked up.

"I guess what bothered me most was your announcing that you were moving to St. Croix. You might have discussed it with me."

"You're the one who says it's better to ask for forgiveness than permission."

That was glib, but we were having a candid conversation. She laughed. "When have you asked my permission for anything? By the way, have you talked to an attorney?"

"No," I said. "Should I? I was hoping we could come to an agreement and avoid lawyers."

Divorce lawyers are dentists of existential angst; with egos like opera divas they gossip like hags; they are made of paper; they bow and scrape before fourth-rate minds who sit on the bench, toadies for a fee, pointing fingers at each other like every pantywaist you hated in the third grade; they are women pinched with animus and fat men who brag to whores, deceitfully wishing to imply gravitas.

"Jason," Margo said, exasperated, "you *need* an attorney."

"Nobody with integrity needs a lawyer."

"That's not the point. Divorce is a legal process; there's money involved; it's a lawsuit; your interest should be protected. I'm not kidding."

In one sense I was charmed that she worried, though I understood it as the practical, perhaps somewhat patronizing advice of a law veteran to an innocent of the courts.

"Call Dirk Boyd, or Marilyn Black, or anyone, but call someone and make an appointment today." Frowning, she lit another cigarette, waving away guilt with her match as she said, "I've retained Ben Issacs."

Ben Issacs?

"Ben? Ben is a friend of ours. Why put him in the middle of our divorce?"

"Divorce is his specialty."

"Divorce is not his specialty; adultery is his specialty; fanning the flames of spousal resentment is his great gift." Margo laughed, and I laughed with her, but it wasn't funny. "Reasonable people don't need lawyers," I insisted, "Aren't we reasonable people?"

"Reasonableness has nothing to do with it."

"Why Ben?" I felt betrayed in a way that was vague and possibly not justified.

"Because he offered to help."

"How kind of him."

Ben Issacs, a natively intelligent man, had that irritating competitive characteristic that must feel superior to everyone at everything. He coached Little League with disturbing vim; he cheated at tennis and golf. I began to wonder if Margo and Ben were lovers but put the thought down as unworthy. In every divorce, disappointments vulgarize the dignity one had hoped to maintain.

"I'll call Marilyn," I said.

"Good. Why not call her now?"

"Because," I said, sharply annoyed, "I'm having coffee and enjoying a certain slant of light in the park, which seems rather cold and stark in this hour, even for autumn."

Margo, single-minded, sighed.

But will had its way eventually. I called Marilyn Black, a friend from college days who specialized in contract law. She worked out an agreement with Ben Issacs. Margo would buy out my share of the co-op. I had three months to find another place to live. This was a technical courtesy, as I had already taken a place in St. Croix. Our belongings and other properties were divided fifty-fifty. It took twenty minutes to read through the agreement, and then we put our signatures on the line at the end.

Later, in civil court, with the same nervous impatience to

finish the ceremony as she'd felt at the wedding, Margo took the stand and swore her enduring commitment to permanent separation. Life reflects with raw precision the sore moment: a gallery of miscreants witnessed our ceremony, whores, junkies, and other vacant-eyed lowlife, so many pronounced frontal lobes and prognathous jaws, such poverty of spirit, so many passively unhandsome faces.

"I hope you understand this is just business," Ben said, as we were leaving the courthouse. "We're still pals, no?"

Ben, Ben, Ben, Ben, Ben.

I felt emotionally swollen, so perhaps I was unfairly judgmental, but I saw Ben as an epic fool, with his yellow tie and brown shoes. I could only view him as a pin-striped ambulance chaser, cynical as a comedian, figuratively snapping twenties and fifties under a light as he listened dispassionately to some desperate client's woe. "Sure, Ben," I said. "We're pals."

Afterward, Margo and I went back to the co-op together. We managed to maintain our humor throughout, which I thought eminently civilized until I began to wonder if we weren't actually in denial about the whole thing. We had, after all, spent ten years together. Oddly, we seemed to genuinely love each other, a sentiment rooted in mutual respect, if never in true chemistry. There was no acrimony at the end, just that sense of time's passage defining something lost.

"Well," she said, standing by the door.

"Well." I touched her cheek and she took my hand and kissed it, this sincere, gentle gesture our last vestige of intimacy, the bittersweet shared final acknowledgment of failure.

"Are you going to be all right?" she said, smiling through authentic tears.

"Are *you* all right?" I answered her question with a question to veil the vulnerability she sensed.

"I'll survive."

"We'll both survive."

I thought I might cry, but I didn't. I stood there remembering our first date, the island and the tepee and the beach, how rich it seemed, how good we felt. I could recall how once, when she smiled, it seemed like sun appearing from behind clouds. In bed I knew a different smile, subdued and mysterious, like the moon's lambency shimmering on the surface of a lake. But that was a dream I had. Now Margo's face was drawn and plaintive and we both felt empty. All the wonder was gone from the world. We were just two lonely individuals, entombed in separate identities, strangers to our future.

part three

An airplane is like a woman.

—hackneyed simile

fifteen

I had come to St. Croix with a vagabond vision: to fly airboats and to make some kind of record of that experience. There was much to say about the romance of the flying boat, and I was moved to write about it. In this I had the good fortune to have a tool at my disposal that I believed was imbued with at least some magic.

About the time I met Charlotte Lansing, I was walking in New York one afternoon and saw a typewriter in the window of a pawnshop, an old black Corona Standard Portable. It caught my eye and piqued my curiosity. The door jingled as I went in. From a far corner, behind a littered desk, the pawnbroker observed me. His reedy voice seemed to leak from the shadows: "Includes the original case."

Squat and plump yet agile in his clutter, he rose to come forward. A black brilliantined hairpiece shone like enameled plastic on his round head. His tiny dark eyes fixed on mine, greeting me with amused suspicion. A pale green tie hung limply against his dingy shirt.

"How old is the typewriter?" I inquired.

"Would you like to see it?"

I nodded. He moved to fetch it from the window display, stepping around empty boxes on the floor, bending over strenuously to get it. He carried it back with a certain reverence, delicately holding it chest high. He put it down gently on the tarnished glass showcase and drew his finger along the handsome gold lettering on its face.

I'd always been a reader, and loved a good clean English sentence, and like someone who can draw capably, I found it satisfying to sketch a scene. I'd kept journals on and off for years, recording names of streets, descriptions of buildings, impressions of people, my own moods, the weather, trying to locate myself in my own experiences.

"A portable machine, the first of its kind, I believe. In an age of complicated things, it's quite refreshing, don't you think?" He smiled and joined his fattish hands at the fingertips, closely watching me. "The greatest writers are fond of these," he said, and then his expression fell and his glance moved off to the middle distance. He sighed. "But excuse me," he said, his eyes finding mine again. "May I ask, sir, are *you* a writer?"

"On some days I think I am."

A flush of unfamiliar pride, like sudden embarrassment, surprised me. He looked down at the Corona Portable and put his fingers flat on the counter near it. "I've been told the right instrument brings inspiration."

I looked around his shop. Rings, watches, carvings, junk jewelry in the display case; a banjo, stuffed birds, a rack of antlers, even a sled hanging on the wall: how did he make a living from that stuff? It mystified me.

"It's a rare model, from the 1940s. It comes with a case, as

I mentioned." He framed the typewriter gently with his fingers, tacitly maintaining possession. Once again his eyes looked down with dissembling humility.

"How much is it?"

"Only twenty-five dollars."

"I'll take it."

He smiled, bowed, and wrote up the purchase receipt.

Maybe the pawnbroker was right about inspiration. I carried the Corona Standard out of the shop believing it was a lucky charm and that something in it could make wishes come true. I didn't realize it at the time, but when I took the typewriter out of the pawnshop I changed my definition of adventure.

One afternoon about a month later, I wandered into the dark neighborhood of the pawnshop once again. It was gone, vanished. At first I thought I'd misremembered the address, but no, I had it right. The store was cleaned out, the walls were bare, some wires sticking out of the floor, that's all, and a pile of junk in the corner. It gave me a strange feeling.

It began as the enjoyment of playing with a toy. The typewriter had none of the work associations I attached to laptops. I liked the feel of the keys, the agreeable sound of letters making words, and the sense I was more directly in touch with experiences of an earlier time. I began with a journal and soon evolved into writing vignettes.

On St. Croix, in Jackson Park, wearing a Panama hat, the Corona Standard Portable perched on its wooden box, I wrote in the shade of palm trees with the soft fragrant breeze off the ocean keeping me cool. The hours passed effortlessly, until the fall of late light on the hills signaled it was time to go home.

As part of my program of change during those first months on the island, I reread some favorite classics, discovering an entirely different experience from what I thought I remembered.

Maturity allowed richer understanding. As I sat by my window at night, a keen sense of life would come to me like a cooling breeze moving through the space of the room. A poetic sentiment began to stir my imagination as it had when I was a child. Often I was moved to spend an hour or two at the typewriter, and afterward a rare peace came that lasted for a short but intensely felt time. I was broaching the artistic impulse.

Aunt Madeline returned to my thoughts in these times of reflection. Madeline was twelve years old when she became my father's stepsister. She was wild and rambunctious, smart and good-looking. Following my father's lead, she learned to fly. Aerobatics were a call of the wild; after college she traveled the country flying air shows. She met and married another stunt pilot, Tom Phillips, and for two years they flew together in a husband/wife routine, but Tom was killed when a loose bolt jammed his controls during a practice flight; Madeline was a widow at twenty-eight. She inherited a substantial sum and retired from professional flying. Literate, skilled, sophisticated, and experienced, she was a hero to me. When one day my parents announced they were taking a vacation in Europe, and, thinking me too young to trust at home alone, made arrangements for me to stay with my aunt Madeline in New York, I was pleased.

"Your father and I think that a change would be good for you. There's nothing for you here while we're away."

"That's right, Son," my father said.

I was sixteen and had begun to notice imperfections in my parents: uneven hues in my father's teeth, a garish tendency in my mother's style of dress. There is no more merciless critic than a thoughtful teenager.

"We'll give you an allowance," my father added, ready with a bribe.

"Madeline will show you all of New York; you'll see and learn wonderful things."

I had never been to Madeline's apartment in New York. I had not, in fact, seen Madeline since she had come to visit with us a year or two earlier, after the death of her husband. By then I had begun to notice her as a woman, and was curious about the inaccessible dimensions of her life. I lurked on the periphery of hushed conversations that she had with my mother, breakfasts prolonged until noon, tea in the afternoon, and finally cocktails outside in the long shadows of evening. I tried to listen, though meaningful conversation stopped abruptly at my appearance. My memory is mainly of heads turning and polite attention that resisted including me. This kept her heroic in my imagination. I wanted to broaden my connection to her, but I was too young; familiar as she was, her personal life remained an entire mystery.

My parents left one day sooner than expected to take advantage of an upgrade. I helped my father load their bags into the station wagon. We said good-bye repeatedly because they kept returning for forgotten items. I couldn't be rid of them quickly enough. I grew restless.

"We'll write," my mother said.

"That's fine," I told her.

"You're going to Madeline's on the morning train?" she asked for the tenth time.

"Yes," I said.

"No friends in the house tonight."

The car began to move. I waved; my mother's hand waved back at me. But the car reached the end of the driveway, then it stopped, *and they came back again.* I stood as they both got out. "Your mother forgot her address book," my father said, in a tone of irritation. I waited on the steps, sitting now, not standing, observing two beetles locked in intercourse on a leaf next to me. I watched them until my mother reappeared for a final effort at departure.

"Good-bye, dear," she said, pinching my cheeks and kissing me yet again, not to appease but to mock my exasperation; there was a wicked comedian under all that hair and makeup. The car moved once more. This time they made it out of the driveway and didn't come back. At last they were gone. I waited on the steps for a few minutes, until the copulating beetles finished their business and took flight; then I went inside and walked through the rooms downstairs, exuberant with solitude. I made a drink and had a cigarette. I went into the living room and listened to music turned up loud, watched television, and masturbated. Later, I ordered pizza delivered. I sampled all of the liquors in my father's cabinet. In the morning, slightly hungover but in excellent spirits, with the optimism of an innocent, I went into the city to see my aunt Madeline's home for the first time.

sixteen

"Good Christ, you've grown up!" Before I could drag my belongings off the elevator she threw her arms around me and gave me a soldier's welcome.

"Hi, Aunt Madeline," I said.

"Drop the 'Aunt,' Jason; we're adults now." She helped me with my bag and then we were standing inside her apartment, where it was large and bright and airy and in a pleasant way confusing for its strangeness.

Madeline had recently turned thirty, and though that seemed near to the grave to me, she was strikingly beautiful. She wore her rose-colored scarf like a turban and sleek black slacks with a white silk blouse. She was Bohemian, insofar as a woman who lives in eight rooms on Park Avenue at 79th Street can be thought of as Bohemian. She took me by the arm and we went inside.

Her living room was vast, with a coffered ceiling and large mirror in a gold frame above the fireplace that gave the room a second accent and deepened the space.

"What can I get you?"

"Nothing."

"Some coffee?"

"I'm fine, really."

She gave me a sidelong glance. "You look a little hungover." I smiled sheepishly.

There was a giant chintz sofa that faced the fireplace, with a great Chinese vase on one side and a potted palm on the other. Green and white brocade fell in neat tucks along the windows. A large painting of what looked like a Roman ruin under moonlight hung on one wall, and I was taken by its subtle colorations. Nothing about the place was stale or dead or cheap.

"Let me show you around." Madeline took me through her home, and each room had some subtle inflection of light and geometry, mood, or composition. The art more than anything—genuine oils, some reproductions, objects, and statuary—arrested my attention. I knew little about art, but I soon discovered that I was affected, even disturbed, by her eclectic collection. Dada lithographs delighted me—urban collages, phallic heads with beaks, disembodied and haunted eyes, expressing antic rebellion. Impressionist, Cubist, Surrealist, and Modern tastes were amply represented in the decoration of my aunt's apartment. I found it exhilarating.

And then there were her books. Wherever there was not art, there were bookcases—books from the floor to the ceiling—in the halls, in the dining room, in the kitchen and the bedrooms, making a mute statement of learning and the life of the mind.

"First get settled, and then come into the study," Madeline said, when we finished the tour. "We'll have a glass of wine, and you can tell me what you would like to see while you're here."

Wine?

She established me in the guest room across from her bed-room, and though it was strange to me, I didn't feel the anxiety that new environments breed. The bed was larger than my own at home and it had a down pad to make it soft. The bedcover was a blue duvet, and the sheets beneath were heavy textured and fresh smelling. I took some time to unpack, arranging shirts, sweaters, socks, and underwear in the dresser drawers, setting up books I'd brought in a stack on the bed table, creating a nest for myself as comfortable and familiar as I could make it.

My aunt was reading a magazine when I rejoined her. The study was a small room, wood walled and filled with books. It had a special atmosphere of intimacy, a smell of leather, and it was agreeably darker in this room than in the rest of the apartment.

"Are you settled?"

"Pretty much."

"Here, try this." She poured us each a glass of red wine from a crystal carafe beside her on a small Florentine table. I took the glass. Raising hers and turning to me, her eyes sparkling with warmth and humor, she made a toast: "To good times." Our glasses touched.

The next morning when I woke, Madeline was sitting at the breakfast table in a pale blue dressing gown, talking on the tele-phone. She waved as I came in, and pointed to a basket of muffins at the center of a table neatly set for two.

"I'd love to, John, really, but I can't," she said. She handed me the morning paper as I sat down.

"No," she said, "Jason is visiting, Jason Walker, my step-brother's son. I told you. . . . Yes. He arrived yesterday."

She wrapped a strand of hair around her finger. "I didn't for-get, but I'll be busy until the weekend after next," she said, curl-ing and uncurling the strand, winking at me. "When you get back. Call me then. . . . Sure; me, too; bye."

She put the phone back in its cradle behind her on the wall

with a practiced toss. The coffee tasted faintly of cinnamon. The room was flooded with morning's full measure of natural light. Sounds from the awakened city rose up from the street in a faint din.

"John wanted to see me tonight, but I had to tell him about the other man in my life." She talked to me over the top of her coffee cup. I was aware of the free movement of her breasts beneath the robe, framed by the tabletop, her arms, and the cup she held to her lips: I had an epiphany: charm is sexual confidence.

"How did you sleep?" she asked, and took a bite of blueberry muffin.

"I had a lot of dreams."

"It means you're stimulated by change. I dream when I travel."

"My dreams never make sense," I told her. "They're like scenes from a lot of movies cut up and put together in a jumble."

"But you remember them?"

"Sometimes." I did not want to pursue this. My dreams of the previous night had featured, among others, Adolf Hitler and a chorus line of Rockettes, naked except for their hats, a psychic floor show I didn't feel inclined to probe.

"I thought we'd take a cab downtown after breakfast," she said. "We can walk around for a while. Follow our inclinations. I think we'll find enough to do."

The city vibrated with sirens, squealing tires, hoots, whistles, and unexplained explosions. Madeline, in black slacks and a sheer white blouse, looked like an ad for perfume. I ambled beside her in a sweater and blue jeans. It had rained during the night, but now the sun was shining and the pavement had that punky smell of evaporating morning damp.

We walked west over to Madison Avenue, home to shops and galleries of premium commerce, then over to Fifth, where grand apartments overlook the park. Madeline raised her hand;

a taxi swerved and stopped in front of us. We climbed into the
roomy backseat. I liked this new world; the faster pace implied
that life mattered.

Madeline observed me surreptitiously. I was watching the
trees in Central Park, vendors along the wall. Then the park
ended. "We'll get out here, driver," she said, handing him his
fare. We started walking west, and then we went south.

We went into a restaurant decorated with potted palm
trees. Sunlight fell across the room, making the scene vivid, and
I watched the waiters moving on the floor between tables, the
maitre d's vexed face disapproving of a loud couple.

"Tell me about your flying," she said.

"I'm about to solo. It's a lot of fun. I remember the stunts you
showed me." I felt on a more equal footing with my aunt, now
that I was learning to fly.

"Don't try those until you have more experience."

"Just remember the three things of no use to a pilot."

"What are they?"

"Altitude above you, runway behind you, and fuel you've used."

The waiter brought us wine and a crab salad. I would never,
I resolved, eat another hot dog.

In the days that followed, Madeline, perhaps without being
aware of it herself, grew more intimate.

One morning she called me into the bedroom.

"Would you bring me the brush, Jason?" The brush was in the
bathroom, and the bathroom was alive with her personal things.
I found the brush and gave it to her. Then I stood behind her
watching in the mirror while she combed it through her hair. "A
hundred strokes," she said, smiling at my reflection.

Meanwhile I noticed that she had become untidy. Her underwear was thrown about. Her robe was loose and almost open.
She seemed not to notice. She asked me again if I had any girl-
friends and then told me I was handsome. All was ambiguous
between us.

In the next few mornings I would appear before her in my underwear when she called for the brush. This became our ritual. I was visibly stimulated and she noticed but pretended not to and yet her eyes met mine often in the mirror and she never told me to leave. Once her robe actually fell open, but only for a brief moment. Our game that had begun in the calm eye of ambiguity moved to ambiguity's edge and then went beyond. We circled each other foraging innuendo for a moment of opportunity, our thoughts jumping.

One night I was reading in the library. It was a hot night; the windows were opened. I heard a key go into a lock and the apartment door opened. Then it closed and I heard the bolt thrown.

"Jason?" She called my name from the kitchen. I didn't answer. She had packages, but I didn't move to help her with them. When she came out of the kitchen I heard her keys fall on the hall table. A book was open in my lap when her face appeared in the doorway.

"There you are." She came into the room. She went over to the window and looked out. She paused there for a moment, and then turned, and she was fanning her face with her hand. "This heat is unrelenting." She said something else, but a siren went by outside and I didn't hear her.

Still fanning her face, she walked over to the couch, and as she moved across the room our eyes became fixed and her hand went slower. I wanted her. I wanted her because she was talented and mysterious, and because I knew that something in the act of sex would change our relationship forever. I didn't know what it was or how it worked, but the sex implied emotional alchemy of some explosive kind, and I wanted to experience whatever it was with someone I knew and admired.

"It's too hot to be civilized. I'm getting out of these clothes. Do you mind?" she said, evaluating my response.

She knew by my stillness and silence that I was inviting her to create the moment. I could not do more than convey somehow that I was discreet, and that I would submit. And so I said nothing, and, significantly, did not move. She sensed consent. Standing right in front of me, she began to unbutton her blouse—first one button, then another, slowly, gauging my response. The book slid from my lap to the floor, ridiculously.

She held her blouse open.

"I want you to watch me," she said. "I want you to enjoy what you see because I enjoy showing it to you. The more you look at me the better it makes me feel."

She lifted her skirt slowly and put one leg on the couch. Her eyes fixed on my expression. She could feel the bewitching magic of her sex fascinate me like a snake charmer who brings a cobra to the point of striking and holds it hypnotized with a flute. Moving even closer, she pulled her skirt entirely up, revealing red silk panties, which she began to stroke and tug and rub and finally pull aside. "Enjoy what you see," she said again, and my fantasies were materializing with the mass and momentum of a steam train.

Then her fingers parted the mysterious cleft. Alive and glistening, so there it was! I slouched beneath it, retreating a bit, I think, at first. A heavy metallic musk breathed from it with intimations of paradise, and I was drawn into the pull of its strange irresistible gravity. I felt worship swell from need. She pulled it apart and held it over me. I stared at it spellbound, and, obeying instinct, fell onto my knees and put out my tongue.

Like a sister-evangelist casting out the devil, she took hold of the back of my head and pressed my face hard into between her legs. Then she threw back her hair and pulled up her bra; her breasts, large and white, with chestnut nipples, moved back and forth above my head in rhythms of what was happening. Somehow we were on the floor, and like the frenzy of snap rolls and spins that were my first introduction to larger possibilities, now she was giving me animal feeling's first taste of sex. In the same way that sensation makes pictures in dreams, so the mind gears up imagination for the mental fires of fantastic voyage. Close your eyes and cling to images that take you at the speed of light to places in your inner space. And now she slides under me, takes hold of my cock, spreads her legs, and puts it in. I groan a little and begin to move, feeling liquid dynamite ignite— weightless, timeless, tumbling through the blue-lit universe inside, dodging dream debris, dancing, whirling, taking giant risky steps through space, laughing like a mad man-angel thumbing his nose at an angry God. I'm gone in deep and she has convulsions, squeezing me inside, and now I'm soaring like Superman over forbidden psychic terrain. Nothing is real, and nothing is what it seems to be: I'm en route through a new universe without meaning meaning everything, where nothing can be believed, a howling place, the psychic underworld where everything is its opposite—pain is pleasure; women, men; courage, fear—where every smile has death in it and every badge of merit commemorates despicable cowardice. Here is where sounds are pictures and solid ground nothing at all. Here the derelict spirit is transformed into an ideal that walks down city streets, and heat-maddened virgins bent over stoops catcall profanities sweeter than a child's prayer. Here is the landscape of every tear, rock-hard and full of concealments. Here the colored ocean of every feeling, affected by every experience, lit from beneath, never still, and in the heat of fucking, the light from beneath, whatever it is, gets bright, but it throws a ghastly shadow up, changing the character of everything that was about to be beautiful into something terrifying, and we take off into space again to go someplace else.

Up and up to the million symbols that cluster where dreams are struck with dystrophy and menace. My aunt shifts and I heave up to look down at what we are about, but the meaning of it disappears, mind and sight disconnect, reason and literacy dissolve into a primitive uncomprehending gape. I am further out of myself than ever before, swimming in sensation, in spastic delirium, disembodied from what is fucking frantically in a different world. A storming moment approaches, and she tears into the flesh of my back until it bleeds, but I'm past-pain and dread, falling now, yawning in spasms that cry remotely, like howls of an infantryman echo as whimpers of denial in that place of neutral reach from which he calmly sees himself commit atrocities.

And now we are soundless and still. Time is absent from the world as we reenter from our separate spheres. I feel blood run down my back. Madeline coos in whispers and turns me over and licks it clean. We lie motionless together on the floor and I feel the rhythm of our breathing calm. Then the sound of traffic in the street returns and I am awake again, but the sound soon fades away and falls in with the confused translations of half sleep. She shifts—and once again I drift up, but only for a moment. Real events melt once again into the fabulous, and now together we drift down into the sightless, soundless, infinitely expanding moment when everything loses its gravity, its meaning, breaks up, floats away, changes into something else, and disappears.

When I was young and had a nightmare, or for some other reason was afraid, my mother would come to me. Then, assuring me in soothing tones, she would take me by the hand into her bed. All fear flew from me. Growling hallucinations, threatening specters, changed at once into vibrations of excited joy. Demons were on a leash, every terror transformed into something radiant. I was invulnerable, protected, flooded with warmth that has security as its ecstasy. This is the moment of pure feeling; we know it once or twice in our lives. This memory of once having known it makes men mad to have it again. For a while we forget about it, but doors of recollection are thrown open as we become crazed with urges. Madeline brought me back to that memory, almost to that feeling. I lay in the darkness with her beside me and I understood why men too far adrift can never have enough money or enough power or enough acclaim, will never find the number of corpses sufficient to put them at ease, and will always be one hair's breadth from a bullet in the brain. It all had to do with that furthest memory. Madeline brought me to a strange reexperience of those first living moments, back into darkness and sensation, to the beginning, to my first awakening as a happy thought in the mind of God.

seventeen

At first I didn't know who she was. In her hat and sunglasses I couldn't see her features, and I had no reason to expect her to be in St. Croix. She was lying on a towel in the sun behind a camel-colored rock near the seawall. I almost tripped over her. Trying to hide my embarrassment, I kept my pace, but I heard her say, "Jason," and out of the corner of my eye I saw her wave. She sat up, then stood, and motioned for me to come over, holding her sunglasses up so our eyes could meet. Hers had a touch of sun-shot gold in them; otherwise they were emerald green.

"Charlotte Lansing," she said, facetiously, extending her hand. Her pupils were dark, making her seem excited and thoughtful. "We've met before."

I laughed. "Yes, I seem to remember."

I thought, How strange that we should meet again here after nearly a year and a half. She wore a yellow blouse open to a white bikini top and white shorts. A welcoming smile formed at the corners of her mouth.

Charlotte sat down on her beach blanket and patted the sand. "Sit a minute, if you can."

I crouched beside her, comparing this sight of Charlotte to my memories: her hair was longer, her smile brighter, her skin tanner, and her full figure still holding claim to youth.

"Surprised to see me?"

"Very surprised."

"Alan bought the house last year. He says tax laws make St. Croix a good investment." Her turned-up face was radiant in the sunlight. "And what brings *you* to this beach?"

"I moved here six months ago. I'm just up the hill on the top floor."

"We're on the point down from you. Is your wife with you?"

"We're divorced."

"Really? I'm sorry—"

"Don't be sorry."

"I hope what happened—," she began, but I waved the comment away.

Charlotte picked up her straw hat with a blue ribbon on it. She put it on and pulled the brim low over her eyes and leaned back on her elbows, legs outstretched and crossed at the ankles.

"Just before I saw you I was wondering why I always feel depraved."

"Depraved?"

"I meant deprived."

"You're baiting me."

Her eyebrows went up in protest, but a smile broke out, betraying her.

On St. Croix in May the sun has desert brilliance. The smell of new life filled the air and the rocks had heat. Her hand swept the line of the horizon. "We should appreciate all this. It doesn't last."

"It lasts," I said. "We don't." I sat, leaned against the rock, and dug a hole in the sand with the heel of my foot. "How have things been?" I asked.

"Pretty terrible."

"Oh?"

"Is it that obvious?"

"Not really."

She began to dig a hole in the sand with the heel of her foot, mimicking me. "How long were you married?" she asked.

"Ten years."

"I've been married eleven . . . twelve years." We gave that number a moment of silence. Charlotte took her hat off and put it beside her on the blanket. "Listen!" she said. "The carnival."

I could hear a calliope, faintly, carried on the breeze.

"Have you seen it? They've set it up on the next beach." There was also distant faint laughter.

"I've seen the roller coaster and the Ferris wheel above the trees."

She sat forward suddenly. "Why don't we go for a ride?"

"On the roller coaster?"

"Come on. It'll be fun." She looked past me, pointing to the woods at the far end. "There's a path through there to the other beach; it's about a quarter of a mile."

I stood and helped Charlotte up. She knotted her blouse, took her sandals and her hat, and left the rest of her things on the blanket. The tide was going out. Children in the water were giggling and splashing.

We went to the wooded path and I held Charlotte's hand where it was steep. In the woods it was dark where we walked, and cool after the bright sun on the sand. I could smell tanning oil on her shoulders. I could smell her heat. I let her hand go, but then I took it again and she turned her head and smiled. The attraction between us was palpable. The path went along the back of a Dutch graveyard. A fieldstone wall surrounded it. The graves were three hundred years old and overgrown with weeds; the tombstones were illegible from erosion. I tried to imagine the early people and their tiny farms along the irregular shoreline. Past the graveyard, the path opened to a marsh where the light was strong again and grasses were green and yellow in the sunshine. Bleached white stones embedded in the wet mud beneath the grasses were dry and bright in daylight that made you squint. After the marsh the path went up once more into a scrub area where a rusted Cyclone fence was violently bent and broken and you could squeeze through it across the property line. We went down again to the beach, and the sand was hot except along the shallow water, where it was cool on our feet. There were many more swimmers at this beach, and sun bathers on beach blankets and colorful beach umbrellas in the sun.

As we walked, a little girl and a man were coming from the other direction. I was going to acknowledge the man with eye contact, but he avoided looking at me as we went past. Charlotte surprised me when she said, "Tell me about them."

I said, "Who?"

"You saw them. What were your impressions?"

All right, I thought.

"The girl at his side is his daughter," I said, "but he's far away in his thoughts. He's recently divorced her mother—say, within the last year—and this is his weekend to have custody. He's not quite sure what the girl means in his life and he can't get past resentment he feels about the situation. He's unable to overcome self-pity to feel his daughter's love. She's needy, but she can't reach him. Add thirty years to the scene, and I see an old, still-unsmiling, still-abstracted figure, an enigma to himself, and a woman bled of spirit and at a loss to explain her failure with men."

Charlotte stopped; an expression of amusement and surprise brightened her features. "I'm impressed," she said.

"It's just a guess."

"But it could be true. It might be true."

I was wondering what sort of a test that was when we got to where the boardwalk began. The boardwalk smelled of tar, creosote, and salt. Some of the wood was splintered, with nail heads protruding in places; the heads were rusted and the windows were weeping rust from corners where salt air had blistered the iron. It saddened me a little to see these fixtures of an older era slowly coming to grief, a mark of time passing. Charlotte was telling me a little about her niece, a nine-year-old girl, and nephew, a boy two years younger. "She has a precocious but arch personality and her father's calculating inclinations. I worry about her compassion." Charlotte's nephew, she said, was avid, full of boyish wildness, charming, sensitive, and loving. "They're good kids."

"Mothers of felons will tell you that," I replied.

She found that comment rich and laughed again. "Why don't you have children?"

I told her that I'd never felt a desire for them, and that perhaps not every adult was meant to be a parent. The subject seemed to evaporate on that comment, punctuated by a silence that followed.

At the entrance to the carnival a fountain shot water high into the air. The fountain was surrounded by a bed of tulips with rainbows hovering above them in the sunlit mist like little miracles. A small boy let a red balloon fly out of his hands. He and his mother watched it ascend above the buildings. Other people turned their heads, and some pointed to it. We walked upwind of the mist and sat on a bench.

"This is a scene I'd like to paint," Charlotte said.

"Are you an artist?"

"Not really. But I love art. I find it relaxing."

The sun was hot. More people collected at the fountain. Everyone seemed a little dazed. The scent of flowers and the sound of birds and children filled the air.

"I like Gauguin," I said. "There's something sinister in the way he combines sex and the devil."

"I went to an exhibition of his paintings last year. There's always a quality of imminence in his subjects. Time is one of his themes, age and youth."

"What do you do with your time?" I asked. "When you're not on vacation."

"I trade stocks."

"Day trading?" I asked.

"I work through three brokerage firms. I spend about five hours a day making trades."

"I think of Wall Street as rabid and voracious."

"And men have the corner on that market?"

I could sense something new in her. She was stronger, more self-assured, less needy. We were both less desperate in our lives.

"How is it working out?"

"The market's a creature that moves this way and that, absorbing, excreting. I'm slowly learning how it thinks. What about you?"

"I retired from business completely. I fly full-time now down here and it's great. I fly the Albatross airboat."

"It's a pretty airplane to see; it must be fun to fly."

"It's a delight. And I've begun to write, something I've always wanted to do. For better or worse I'm trying to do all those things we tend to put off."

The wind took a strand of hair to her mouth and she brushed it away. As if on a signal we rose from the bench and walked to the edge of the boardwalk where the wash of waves mixed with carnival sounds.

"Writers have opinions. What do you think about sexual addiction?" she asked suddenly.

"Not much," I told her. "Americans want a twelve-step program for everything that frightens them about being human."

"If it interferes with your life or your job, isn't that the defini-tion of addiction?"

"Sleep interferes with everything. Am I addicted because I re-quire sleep at regular intervals?"

"Then why is everyone so screwed up about it?"

"Passion is unruly."

"Who makes this shit up?" she said.

"People who fear their instincts."

"Alan is a fearful man." Charlotte looked away. "He always seems on the verge of panic, but he tries to hide it." She turned again to face me. "What do you fear?"

"Loneliness. And you? What do you fear?"

"Irrelevance."

We went back along the boardwalk past the fountain where the creosote scent of the docks changed into esplanade smells of hot dogs, fresh paint, and pavement. I could hear the calliope sound of the carousel, and laughter of people on the silver rocket ride. The last hour had unfolded effortlessly, with plea-sure. Without being especially coy, she had probed my sensibili-ties, and I could sense the nuance in her mood, which is not to say I could read her thoughts; on the contrary, I felt she could read mine. I was about to say something when a voice at some distance behind us called:

"Charlotte!"

She stopped and turned in the direction of the voice, a look of incredulous annoyance coming over her all at once.

"Charlotte!"

He came at us in jaunty hale strides, waving cheerfully in his green polo shirt, silver hair combed back and a gray mustache. Good looks had lost their vitality to drink, but there remained a certain natural athletic trim, a generic even-featured hand-someness of the aging golf pro or the not-yet-outed television game show host. A little out of breath, full of bright false cheer, and wearing the guilty grin of a man caught red-handed in a petty theft, Alan Lansing slowed his pace and sauntered up to us.

"Alan," said Charlotte. "What are you doing here? I thought you were working at home."

Avoiding her question, he turned his eyes on me with suspicious curiosity. "And you're . . . ?" He feigned vague recognition.

"Jason Walker," I said. He knew who I was, and he knew I knew he knew it.

"Oh sure," he said, faking good cheer. He shook my hand with the corporate death grip that goes on competitively to a defeat or a draw. Charlotte watched him silently for a long interval, letting awkwardness envelop him until he began to seem ridiculous.

"I saw Bruce Avery on the docks," he said, turning to me as he spoke. "Amy's back. He wants us to join them for cocktails."

"You followed me here to tell me that?" Charlotte heaved an angry sigh and looked away from him.

"You told me you'd be at the beach."

"He reconstitutes reality when it's convenient." They were talking to each other through me. Charlotte's tone was cold. "I'm not at the beach, Alan; I'm at the carnival. With Jason. You followed me."

"For heaven's sake."

"*You followed me.*"

"Rick doesn't want to hear this. We can talk about it later."

"His name is Jason."

"I'll tell Amy we're meeting them." He drew his pocket cell phone like a weapon.

"Don't do that here," Charlotte said.

Alan looked at her with real anger; a tortured smile ironed itself back on.

"I'll tell you what," he said. "I've got a ton of things to do. Why don't you finish your walk with Rick—I'm sorry; Jason—and I'll see you back at the house later."

"You know, Alan, after the New Year's Eve party you couldn't get his name out of your mind. Jason Walker. Surely you remember. You screwed him out of the Maine camp."

"Nice to see you, Jason." Alan seized my hand once again with a glaze of good cheer supervening his anger; then he turned to Charlotte. "Toodles," he said.

Toodles?

"Do you see what just happened?" Charlotte said bitterly when he was out of earshot.

"I'm not exactly sure. Was he really following us?"

"Oh yes. Because I'm leaving him."

"Does he know it?"

"I told him last month. Spying is his way of being desperate."

"You haven't separated?"

"The divorce is set for August. We're trying to be civil about it. We have the house down here and he wanted a last vacation. I agreed. That was probably a mistake. He can't accept it."

I thought of Margo and Paris: the ceremonials of disengagement can be torturous.

"I'd rather you hadn't mentioned New Year's Eve."

"I wanted to hurt him. I'm so tired of his insanity."

"Does he know about us?"

"He knows about New Year's Eve. I thought he knew more, but I don't think he does."

Past is past, I thought, and let it go at that.

It was a bizarre encounter nonetheless, and the earlier mood was shattered. We gave up the roller coaster and started back past the marsh, through the woods behind the cemetery, finally to the small beach where I had first seen her.

When we got back to her blanket, she took my hand. "Don't go just yet." She lay down on her blanket and I sat back against the camel-colored rock. The tide was higher; the sand spit where children had been playing near the breakwater was completely submerged. A wind began to blow, and the waters offshore darkened with it. Sailboats heeled on a close reach, their sails slicing the air at a steeper angle, and sometimes they seemed about to collide. Charlotte put on her straw hat and sunglasses and leaned back on her elbows, the same reclining pose I had found her in, thoughtful, facing the horizon, silent, alone.

"Do you feel the attraction between us?" she said.

"Of course."

"It's still there, strong as ever, isn't it?"

I nodded.

"If I knew you better would I like you less?"

"I like to think not."

"I'm feeling vulnerable right now," she said, her aspect falling. "I'm wary of everything."

She took my hand into hers and squeezed it affectionately. We exchanged phone numbers. "I'll call you soon," she said, and I left the beach wondering what, if anything, had changed in my life in the last two hours.

It was a walk of a little less than a mile to Christiansted. I went through nearby hills where trees along the sidewalks were thick with leaves, grasses were trim, and the properties were flattered by flowers and fragrances of spring. I walked past the hedges and iron gates surrounding great estates where carefully groomed lawns were landscaped with mysteriously wonderful refinements. White butterflies flitted like fairies on honeyed air; dogwood rained yellow blossoms on the trim green grass; bumblebees hovered in pink bougainvillea and there were birds in the trees, strawberries in the garden, and everywhere a scent of flowers and fruit. I paused covetously, finally dismissing the glamour of wealth as a myth while yet somewhat chagrined that I belonged to a species not immunized against the necessity to shop and do laundry.

I stopped at the post office to check my mail. It was the time of day for errands before evening, and a number of women were shopping the grocery and liquor stores in tennis dress. I went to the Comanche for a glass of wine. Men at the bar drinking beer had been sailing. Their heads were sunburned; they bantered with friendly jibes and twice-told jokes. I sat down and ordered from the bartender, relaxing in agreeable social solitude, recalling the day, and thinking it would be fun to take Charlotte for a flight sometime. She'd like flying; she'd like the freedom of it; her manner with me welcomed unique experience as an intimacy to be shared, and the Albatross was a unique experience. Her scent came back to me. Her husband's strange grin flickered in my mind. He looked deranged. Behind his dissembling of my name was keen anger. Imagine the surprise he must have felt when he saw me once again with his wife; sex unhinges men. Fuck him, was my final thought. I had a second glass of wine and returned to my rooms in a brilliant mood.

eighteen

The hull of the Albatross touched down gently, slapping across the waves; it slowed and settled into the water. As we neared the shore I put the landing gear down and steered to the ramp. When the nosewheel made contact with the concrete incline I gave the engines a blast of power and we went up the ramp. I turned to face the ocean and shut down the engines.

Jack Hibbard shook my hand. "Congratulations. You did a great job. This completes your Captain's checkride." He had a big smile on his face.

The ground crew was waiting as we deplaned, three young Cruzian boys ready to give the ship a freshwater bath. Jack gave them instructions while I tidied up the cabin.

We walked along the boardwalk to Stixx, a bar with a broad view of the harbor. Yarrow Thompson was bartending and she gave us a big smile as we sat down.

Jack ordered two Heinekens.

She grabbed two mugs and filled them to spilling.

Yarrow was about thirty, fair-haired and deeply tanned, with that square-faced handsomeness of athletic women that gains character with age. Her legs were strong. Her eyes were pale blue, and she had a warm, engaging smile. Her charm had its roots in her self-sufficient nature; she was humorous and direct; she could laugh at a bad joke without pretending it was a good one; people liked her. Yarrow was a local free floater, part of the ongoing migration of young people drawn to the islands each year who arrive for one season and stay on for several. She'd worked at almost every restaurant and bar in Christiansted and had an unofficial seniority; her industry and reliability made her a kind of universal employee among the managers and charter companies in town.

"Jason's now Captain of the *American Clipper*," Jack said to Yarrow as she put our beers down.

"Congratulations." She put down three shots and filled them with whiskey. "Here's to blue skies, tailwinds, and not landing before you plan to." We toasted to that, which amused Jack tremendously.

I was in a great mood. Jack had hired Johnny Buehn to fly with me in the right seat more or less permanently. Johnny was in his late twenties. He was a strong pilot and a good mechanic, too, who wrote poetry and hated to wear shoes. He and his brother, Rob, had come down from the Delaware Bay, where both had been brought up sailing. Rob had a sailing school and managed charters. He had a philosopher's mind for the mysteries of the horizon, while Johnny had a flyer's poetry in his heart.

"You and Johnny can make it work," Jack said.

Yarrow was listening. "If you ever need a mate, I'm available," she said.

"We just might." I turned to Jack, nodding in her direction. "Yarrow occasionally works sailing charters."

"Keep her in mind. You'll be doing charters soon. Find an island beach not too far off; the operating costs are small, but the
clients get to spend the day with the airboat. People love it and
it's profitable."

"What got you interested in flying boats, Jack?"

He smiled. "Flying boats landing in these harbors is like a
beautiful dream come true. Juan Trippe and Charles Lindbergh
started airboat travel in the Caribbean. Soon flying boats were
taking passengers and cargo across the oceans. Everything
seemed possible; real heroes made aviation happen. I wanted to
be part of the dream."

"Let's toast to old real heroes and old best dreams."

Jack raised his glass.

"To the imagination and dreams of those who came before
us; to our own dreams; and to those who succeed us, may their
dreams come true."

nineteen

In June of that year Margo married her lover. She called to let me know, which I thought decent of her, but it was hard news to hear.

I flew to New York once each month to get my mail and take care of stray errands. It was an easy flight and kept me free from island fever. In New York for a weekend, I happened to run into Margo and her new husband one Sunday afternoon at Chumley's, in Greenwich Village. They were sitting together at the end of the bar when I walked in. Chumley's started as a speakeasy in the 1920s; the walls are papered with book jackets of writers who drank there; it's a place I often went to when I was in town. Margo, in shock, introduced us. "This is Brad," she said. Ludicrously, I insisted we have a glass of wine together. Overcoming reluctance, Margo agreed. I joined them. Brad was a lawyer.

"I understand you're retired," he said.

"From the business world, anyway."

"Margo told me you had an antique Beechcraft."

"It's not really an antique." I didn't want to get into a discussion about flying with Brad. Instead I wanted to tell Margo that I was making real progress on a book, but the epic lameness of such a claim in this context made that subject pointless and impossible.

"You know what they say," Brad said. "No one should feel sorry for anyone who owns his own airplane."

I looked at him with a questioning expression.

We talked, inanely. Brad and I had little in common. Brad was a golfer; I'm not. Brad liked sports cars; I don't. Brad had a pierced ear; I didn't. Brad seemed inordinately fit, and I don't know why that should have struck me as ridiculous, but everything about him annoyed me in some way: his black turtleneck sweater (in June!), his giant gold watch; and he kept touching Margo possessively, like a forest primate. She, who knows how I think, asked me to forgive him with her eyes. A glass of wine never took longer to finish.

At last the check came, I paid it, and Brad said that he and Margo were going to an off-off-Broadway play. "The son of one of my partners wrote it. It's about lesbians," he said, winking. We shook hands insincerely. Margo gave me a generous hug and I sensed a new bond. Even if, at the end, our parting had been a relief to both of us, we had borne witness to ten years of life together. Our try at happiness had failed, but there would always linger in the face of time's passing a mutual respect, and a resolve that those years had not been spent in vain.

Madeline and I shared the same rogue gene. Over the years we corresponded with regularity, and once a year, usually between Thanksgiving and Christmas, we spent a day and sometimes a night together for old times. It became our family tradition, you might say, a holiday we gave ourselves from the cares of daily living, so before returning to St. Croix I phoned her to see if she could meet me for Sunday brunch.

"Fabulous," she said. "Why don't we meet at the Mark at one thirty."

The Mark Hotel on East 77th Street is not far from her apartment; it has elegance and privacy, a perfect place for quiet conversation and catching up. I arrived early, got our table, and ordered a glass of Burgundy. The main room has two windowless levels done in cool colors of green and rose, and pillars for added charm. The waiter arrived with my wine. When Madeline appeared at the entrance, I stood; she saw me, waved, and came over. There were two couples on the other side; we were in the corner on the second level and the tables nearby were empty.

"You look wonderful," she said, as we embraced.

"And you've lost ten years."

She waved away a flattery, but I meant it. Madeline had maintained her lean good looks; she'd kept fit; her eyes were youthful and without lines; her waist was narrow and her breasts were as full and voluptuous as ever. Dressed in black slacks and a white cotton pullover, she seemed an older version of her younger self, retaining those attractive attributes of character so becoming to women of a certain age.

We sat. She quickly surveyed the dining room, settling in. She ordered a glass of Bordeaux from the waiter, who bowed slightly and withdrew.

"When did we see each other last?" I said.

"You don't remember?" She feigned chagrin.

"A little more than a year ago, I think."

"You and Margo were still together. How is Margo?"

"Married, as a matter of fact."

"Really?"

"I met her and her new husband just yesterday, bumped into them accidentally."

"And?" Madeline rested her chin on the back of her hand and smiled.

"He's a bit of an ass, but he seems to care for her."

"You're cold," she said, amused.

"I was cordial," I protested. "They're right for each other. He's a lawyer; they speak the same language—with forked tongues."

"I always liked Margo," said Madeline, reaching for her glass, her expression serious, "but I couldn't feel passion there. You, on the other hand, are passionate and fond of adventure."

"I feel the loss," I said.

I must have sounded gloomy; Madeline took up my part. "Jason, you don't like to feel you've hurt anyone. There's nothing wrong with Margo or with you; she wasn't on your wavelength. She's pragmatic; you're whimsical. I'm sure you got on each other's nerves. Tell me about St. Croix."

"It's better than I thought it would be."

"What's the island like?"

"Changing. The economy is getting stronger. Tax incentives are bringing in investment. Half the places are showing neglect, and half are being refurbished. The bars are good, people are happy, and I'm having fun."

"You're flying the Grumman Albatross?"

"I just made Captain as a matter of fact."

"I never did fly seaplanes. I was too into flying upside down."

"Do you fly now and then?"

"Maybe twice a year I'll go up with friends."

"But you were so good. You loved it."

"After Tom died, something went out of it for me. I still love it, but I have a different life now; I had a lot to prove to myself; I don't feel that way anymore."

A couple came into the dining room holding wet umbrellas.

"Any romance in your life?" she asked.

"I've met somebody. Or met again."

"Really?"

"Her name is Charlotte Lansing."

"I know the name."

"Her husband is Alan Lansing."

"Isn't he an investor who was in some trouble not long ago? I seem to recall an investigation."

"He's managed to stay in the shadows, but yes, he's been behind some of the notable bankruptcies of the last five years. He lurks; he hovers; we had to pay him a greenmail fee to keep him out of our merger."

"You know, there's something else about him," Madeline said, holding her finger to her lips. "His name comes up at cocktail parties sometimes. It seems to me I heard he owns a production company in Canada that makes adult films."

"I hadn't heard that."

Madeline sipped her wine thoughtfully. "I've never cared much for men who crave money and power; they're always strange in bed. I dated one CEO who asked if he could call me Miss Buckley and pretend he was in grade school writing his ABCs. He never got the *W* right, so I was supposed to whack him on the knuckles with a ruler."

"And?"

"He'd come, right at his little desk."

"His desk?"

"He had a room in his apartment done up like the third grade."

"You're kidding!"

"Jason, you don't see what women see; men are a very troubled species. I dated a district attorney once who liked being led around on a leash. I'm warning you, this Alan Lansing fits the profile. I wouldn't be surprised if he barked and yelped himself to climax in adult diapers."

"He's got this weird spying thing with Charlotte. She and

I met on the beach in the most coincidental way, and suddenly he was on the scene."

"Be careful of him. He can't be thrilled about you and his wife; you may be wearing a target."

I shrugged.

"I mean it, Jason. You tend to think everybody thinks about life more or less the way you do. I've got news for you: your feet don't touch the ground. Keep your eyes open, is all I'm saying."

Madeline, suddenly remembering something, raised her finger. "I came across a feature in a magazine the other day and thought you'd be amused at Wilbur Wright's dry wit." She reached into her purse, took out a folded page, and read from it:

" 'On Thursday, October 27, 1910, Arch Hoxley, a twenty-six-year-old exhibition pilot trained by the Wright brothers, took off from Belmont Park on Long Island to set a new altitude record. The winds above a thousand feet were strong out of the west, and Hoxley could make no headway against them; on the contrary, astonished spectators watched him disappear to the east, tail first, at full throttle. Reporters asked Wilbur Wright what he thought about the unforeseen spectacle. "Just one straightforward progress, backwards," he said.' "

"I hope that's not the story of my life," I laughed.

The waiter appeared and we ordered lunch.

twenty

I returned to St. Croix eager to pick up my routine again. Flying is always a joy, and when work goes well at the typewriter life takes on a luminous aspect. But writing is unpredictable, and there are days when the mind won't awaken. On this particular day the work had been thoroughly unsatisfying; it just wasn't there anywhere. I'd slept deeply but awakened weary, with a vague sense of loss. My dreams had been anxious, but I was unable to remember them. I tried to write but couldn't concentrate. As the hours passed without accomplishment I began to have that writers' worry of I don't know anything, I'm not making productive use of my time, life is passing me by, and for such vain waste there will be no second chance, no redemption, no distinction, no book, no epitaph, nothing.

I was ready to give up on the afternoon when Charlotte

phoned. I hadn't expected to hear from her so soon. The sound of her voice broke the gloom of my mood.

"I want to see you where we can be alone."

"You know where I am," I told her. "Come over in an hour."

I was glad she'd called; I waited in my chair by the window with happy anticipation.

I began to think hard about our earlier affair; it all came back to me: I was deep in daydreams when she knocked on the door at the bottom of the stairs. I called down to her. The early-afternoon sun was shining brightly, and when the door opened bright light filled the stairwell so that Charlotte seemed to walk out of it as though materializing from my thoughts of her.

She was wearing a white filigree Indian cotton blouse with long billowing sleeves, and blue shorts. Her hair was pulled back loosely in a single braid and her eyes, always striking, seemed particularly bright. There was a sonorous quality to her voice with an erotic nuance that didn't pronounce a name so much as announce an experience she wanted to have: "Jason," she said. She was brimming. Her skin smelled sweet, like rainwater or fresh fruit. We kissed with the familiar passion.

She stepped back to survey my modest apartment. Though small, the room had a distinct charm, and I was rather proud of its composition: the books in two mahogany bookcases made a mute statement of intellectual engagement; photographs of fly-ing boats spoke of early airliners and told of airborne romance; three wooden African masks, of adventure; a primitive lute, that music was part of civilized living; and of course the Corona Standard Portable, my tool of trade. A soldier needs his guns about him, the religious man his amulets; these were my objects of comfort, my metaphors, my few good things.

"I feel you in here," she said, with obvious approval.

"Would you like some wine?"

I had her sit at the table while I got two glasses from the small cabinet above the sink. She studied the view of the harbor where the sailboats drifted at their moorings. "Do you write here at the window?"

"Right where you're sitting."

"And you use that old typewriter?" The typewriter was on the floor in the corner by a stack of manuscript pages.

"Its sound consoles me."

She smiled. A bar of bright sunlight lay diagonally across the floor. I handed Charlotte her glass of wine and sat in the chair opposite her at the window.

"I've been thinking about you," she said. She ran her finger around the base of the wineglass. She was gazing at the harbor when her cell phone rang.

"I'm sorry." She took the phone out of her bag, read the ID, frowned, turned it off, and threw it back. "Alan," she said.

Alan, embottled genie, wished to be summoned, but Charlotte refused the rub, keeping him in that limbo of the unanswered. Then she smiled, reached for my hand, squeezed it, and sipped her wine thoughtfully. The room was bright with sunlight. She was comfortable, with that happy eagerness when anticipation yields to an actual event.

"Yesterday I was thinking how little I understand about average things."

"You're not alone."

"How does a voice go through space, for example? What makes a radio work? And what does any technology end up meaning?"

"It's supposed to make life easier."

"Do you think it does?"

"What things do and what they mean are different questions. Take a radio," I said. "There are two things to consider about a radio; the science that sends a voice through space, and the effect of the voice on people who listen to what it says."

"Where's the meaning in any of it?"

"Each of us decides. Is the Internet a useful tool or a multi-layered distraction? Some use it for research, or to meet other people. Others use it to escape; browsing sedates them. Different strokes."

"What do you think about hypocrisy?" she asked.

"What about it?"

"Is it a good thing or a bad thing?"

"Neither. Hypocrisy is like a white lie; it's a necessary convention."

"A lie is a lie."

"That's narrow understanding. White lies are like oil in machinery; they're expedient, and we understand that, and their acceptability has something to do with what interest is served in telling them. Therefore, context matters, just as it does with hypocrisy."

"Where's the line?"

"There is no line. With hypocrisy it's a matter of degree: if you have too much, you're a politician; too little, you're a psychopath."

A broad smile broke out on her face. I viewed her abrupt inquiries, something I'd noticed when we were together on the beach, as flattery to my understanding of things.

"It must be pretty for you in the mornings here, to sit by the window alone." She continued to look out at the view. She paused, turned to me. "It's an achievement that you've changed your life in the ways you have. It seems a simple thing, but I know it isn't; it's painful and difficult."

"Life passes too quickly. I had to make changes."

"I'm making changes."

"I know."

"It frightens me."

Silence settled between us as though we were having the same thought. I was getting a good feeling about Charlotte again and it made me worry. Gamblers get a feeling about a number or a horse. Feelings are the least reliable component of certainty.

She took my hands, pressing them into hers. We looked at each other with that thrill of emotions making pleasure from tensions that otherwise cause pain.

I led her to the other side of the room. I could feel her vibration, something terribly alive. We tumbled into bed. She lay on her side with her head turned up and her shoulders thrown back, watching my eyes.

"I'm so lonely." She sighed deeply, turning her head to look away.

"We're together; it's all right; you're here with me."

"I'm afraid of loneliness."

She closed her eyes. "The world seems very dark sometimes," she whispered, "and I know it's not the world at all."

I held her close to me; her hands ran along my body like a blind girl with a man in her arms for the first time. We made love slowly, sharing sensations in desire's timeless and absolute moment. Yet we were less frantic now, with a different understanding, less urgent, more intimate. Holding her, I tried to understand the myriad expressions of love, the fleeting nature of exaltation, and why average life is so often felt to be a sum of unaccommodated needs when it should be much more than that.

Charlotte sat by the window wearing my Chinese robe. Disheveled hair against the sun made an aura that lit the symmetry of her features in a dark golden glow; her beauty was shocking, blazoned, divine. I went to her at the window. She reached out to touch me. Smiling broadly, she took my hand and squeezed it gently. "I better go," she said.

When she dressed I walked her down the stairs into the truthful light of afternoon; she was radiant as a saint. "I'll call you soon," she whispered, and then she was gone, like a day-dream.

Love never happens in the ways you expect, and it seems to require living beyond means. Who was she, who had come into my world like this for the second time? I went back to the table and looked out the window a little nervously, with that sense of life impending, like a gambler who's borrowed a large sum of money he can't pay back without luck.

twenty-one

"We create what we need from the wreckage of what we've lost,"
I said.

"That's clever understanding, mate." The man sitting next to
me raised his bottle to salute agreement.

"Not always, but often; not in all things, but always in matters
of the heart."

"More often than is good or sound." He shrugged with his
eyebrows as he tipped up the bottle and had a sip of his beer.
Then he put the bottle down and extended his hand. "Mitch
Holden, by the way."

"Jason Walker." We shook hands. "I've seen you around."

"I'm a journalist for a rag in Brisbane, here on vacation."

"I fly the airboat."

"Bloody Hell!" he said. "It's a pretty sight when you land in
the harbor."

Close to my age, he had blond rugged good looks, with a sailor's skeptical blue eyes and an antic Aussie sense of humor. He lived aboard his ketch, *Threshold*, anchored in the harbor, and I was happy to have a chance to meet him. We were talking about love, about women.

"How do you imagine a woman, mate? That's the question. And how does she imagine you? Because, you see, a relationship is an ongoing daydream."

"I haven't heard that before."

"It's true enough. Think of it."

I had the day off and had walked to the Comanche for a drink and lunch. It had begun to rain. The rainfall was heavy and gave a fresh, clean smell to the air.

"Let me get this round." He motioned to the bartender, who nodded, put down two fresh bottles, and took away the finished ones.

I told Mitch about Charlotte. "But you can't mention this to anyone," I said. "She's divorcing her husband and I don't want to gum up the works."

"I've met him."

"Her husband?"

"Alan Lansing."

"Where?"

"On the golf course; he cheats."

"I'm not surprised," I laughed.

Mitch shrugged. "Serious players don't take it lightly."

The rain was hard now and you couldn't see Protestant Key. There wasn't any wind; it poured steadily. Mitch had begun to tell me about a woman named Mira who had turned his head. A cynic is a spoiled romantic often enough, and I wanted to see how hard-boiled he really was.

"You were going to tell me about the European woman. Who was she?"

"She was a figment of my imagination."

"Did you love her?"

"She agitated fugitive desires."

"You're equivocating. Were you intimidated?"

"Maybe. I worshiped her. She made me feel holy, but like everything about her it was an illusion; piety has no place in the part of the soul she touched." He stared distractedly at the label on his bottle. "She had desperate passions."

"Where did you meet her?"

Mitch toyed with his bottle. "I first saw her in New York," he told me. "I was working on a feature about music in the great cities."

"Sounds like a perfect assignment."

"I try." He smiled slyly. "The editor thought it was a good idea, so off I went. There is a café in New York, on Broadway near Columbia, where they play jazz on Sundays after brunch. I was at the bar and she was across the room with her back to the wall in the far corner. The music was exceptionally good, the moody impressionism of Thelonious Monk, the mournful joy of Louis Armstrong. A soprano saxophone played Armstrong's trumpet licks through 'West End Blues.' I noticed her looking at me; the dark room amplified her eyes.

"After the set, I introduced myself. Her name was Mira. She was European, from Germany, a small village called Barntrup, in the north. We talked. I learned she was unable to leave her apartment after dark. 'I'm afraid at night,' she said. It was rare, she told me, that she would come to a place so full of people, so like the night, so far from her own neighborhood. I was intrigued.

"We made a date for lunch. She canceled four times at the last minute using different excuses. I was about to give her up entirely when she called and promised not to disappoint me. She came in evening dress, a black silk skirt, nylon stockings, and high heels, a natural beauty, but one thing she said during our conversation gave me pause: 'I hate myself.'

"We dated chastely twice. When I told her I wasn't keen on where I lived, she immediately offered me her apartment, just like that. 'I'm going back to Germany for a few months,' she said. 'It would work for me to have someone staying at my place while I'm away.' Her offer came at a crucial moment. I had been renting a room in a marginal neighborhood and I needed a change. I took her up on it."

Mitch cocked his head thoughtfully to one side. His eyes narrowed as though trying to bring memory into clearer focus.

"She left for Europe and I moved my few belongings into her one-bedroom apartment. Her possessions, her life, was here, exactly as she'd left it. I was suddenly a part of that life; my things were intermingled with hers; I slept in her bed, between her sheets, my head on her pillows. My identity was superimposed on hers; I had awakened from my life into hers."

Mitch paused and looked reflectively at rainwater pouring from gutters on the narrow street below. He turned to me again and I saw something new in his eyes; he was thoughtful and deeply intelligent.

"I have never had the fetish impulse, yet all at once I began to be curious about this other person and her personal effects. Perhaps I was emotionally depleted and vulnerable to fantasy. I could feel her contours, her sexuality, her spirituality. Her soul was troubled, she suffered from depression, she had obsessions, but she also had a pure spirit and high intelligence."

Mitch had a sip of his beer. He turned his head to look at me directly. "All her books, philosophy, psychology, self-help books, were underscored. Reading them was like reading her autobiography.

"After a time," he continued, "I wanted to see her. We had talked about my coming to Germany. We had agreed on sometime in October. I had gone to London to visit an old friend, thinking I would call from there, and continue on to Barntrup if I sensed a sincere invitation.

" 'Will you come to visit us, then?' she said brightly.

" 'Yes,' I said. 'I'll fly to Hannover on Saturday and come by train.'

"So I went. When I saw her she was radiant, so naturally full of life, a picture of health, her face more attractive than I remembered, her body slender and strong, her eyes shining brightly with warmth and allure. I didn't shake her hand; rather I instinctively brushed her cheek gently with the back of my fingers, holding them there for a certain interval as we looked into each other's eyes.

"After a minute of greetings chat, she said, 'Tell me about the apartment; are you comfortable there?'

" 'Very.'

" 'There are no problems?'

" 'Your superintendent was not happy to see me at first. Your lease forbids sublets.'

" 'He can be an asshole.'

" 'I made friends with him. Everything's all right.'

" 'Would you like to go for a walk in the morning?'

" 'I'd love to,' I said.

" 'The forest is not far.'

"The forest, right out of a bloody fairy tale. 'I'd like that,' I said.

"I was waiting for her in the morning when she came down to breakfast; she looked at my feet. 'You'll have to change your shoes,' she said. After we finished she said, 'I'll get Sonny.'

"Her dog was a brown mixed-breed bitch with a playful disposition, but I was bloody hungry to be alone with Mira; she had been by turns shy, fearful, circumspect, welcoming, and wary with me. I didn't know where I stood.

" 'Will these do?' I said, pointing to leather walking shoes, wondering if boots were better suited.

"She turned to see them. 'Those are fine,' she said, and put on her scarf, then pulled a wool hat low over her brow and looked at her reflection in the hall mirror.

"The temperature was on the chilly side, but the land was steep and we'd be keeping a pace; she wore a sweater.

" 'Ready?' she said. I nodded. She looked past me to the dog, who came charging down the stairs with happy-dog delight that makes you laugh out loud. 'Sonny, Sonny, Sonny, beeshsa, beeshsa, beeshsa.' She bent over, rustling the dog's ears vigorously, speaking to her in German, which I don't understand except as glottal and fricative sounds. When the three of us went outside, Sonny ran ahead.

" 'The forest is only just across the street,' Mira said.

"I followed her on a path that quickly narrowed, and within minutes I was lost in the woods.

" 'This is where I came as a child to play. I'll show you.'

"I studied the back of her as she walked. She was thin and tall and she was wearing a stretch fabric that revealed strong muscles in her thighs, a body that was tight and lean. She walked in even strides, a confident gait that showed she was familiar with the path that almost disappeared at times as it went down steeply and then around and up through thicker woods. The leaves had not yet turned. The sky was blue and bright through the canopy, but the woods stayed agreeably dark where we walked. She began to talk about her illness.

" 'I have bad days, but it's getting better. The medication has already been reduced. I'm going to start therapy here soon, and that will help.'

"Halfway up, where the woods were thicker, she stopped and pointed to what looked like the ruin of a fireplace, or a shrine of some kind. It was a semi-circle of brickwork with a crumbling concrete base built into the rising ground.

" 'I used to come here; it seemed to have significance, but I never knew what it was for.'

" 'It's where virgins were sacrificed to Goths,' I told her. She laughed.

"We kissed by her shrine; that was all: one deeply felt kiss. I left her with that unappeased desire, a passion for possession that some psychologists call the threshold of love."

Mitch finished his beer and ordered another round for us. A complicated look came over him.

"Her disrobed body was discovered shortly after my return, hypothermia at the shrine she had shown me ten days earlier."

"Dead?"

"Suicide." His eyes retreated into abstraction. "She had a relationship with the world like night wind. She had drugged herself. She left a final note, indicating a personal effect that I should receive. When it arrived, I opened the package and un-wrapped . . . her lipstick. It was my turn to be surprised. Recall-ing my first sight of her, I thought of Armstrong's 'West End Blues' as a dirge now."

Mitch looked at me with a boozy smile, joyful and chagrined. "So what do think, mate?"

"I don't know."

He slapped his fist down adamantly. "Mine was the delusion of a lonely heart; hers was a failure of imagination: loneliness in both cases, nothing more. If loneliness can't be overcome, the world is distorted and the people you meet in it have a sickness. She didn't know who she was."

We sat together in a meditative silence for several minutes. Mitch was an interesting person. Men will brag about their sex-ual prowess, but he was at a different level with emotions. When you live on a boat, I thought, large questions of the world don't answer the greater needs of spirit.

The rain ended. The dark rain clouds dissipated and the sun began to appear intermittently. It made the air hot and humid.

"It was a pleasure to meet you, Mitch," I said. "I look forward to friendship."

"Likewise, mate; likewise, to be sure."

I went home at odds with the sunshine, walking along the docks, a little drunk and downhearted about loneliness and laughter and suicide and smiles.

twenty-two

"Hello, Jason? This is Alan Lansing. . . . Charlotte's husband, that's right. How are you? . . . Good. Listen, Charlotte asked me to give you a shout. I'm calling because we're having a few people over for cocktails tomorrow evening. . . ."

His intonation was unctuous. I did not believe that Alan Lansing wanted me there; I felt Charlotte's insistence behind it. Curious, though, I decided to go; when I arrived, Alan greeted me like an old school chum.

"Glad you could make it, Jason," he said, seizing me with his death grip. Wearing a blue blazer and white ducks, Alan looked like new money pretending to be old.

Their home, a renovated sea captain's house, was impressive. Tax incentives made it no surprise that a community of speculators had migrated from the States. The Lansing home stood at the end of Rocky Point peninsula. A wide glass face offered a spectacular water view. A flagpole with yardarm and gaff at the point suggested a ship under way. The setting sun, red and gigantic, shone below the clouds, projecting a purple-orange conflagration somewhere distant. I paused for a moment on the porch to study the spectacle.

"It's a beautiful view," I remarked.

"Charlotte's inside somewhere," Alan said, holding the door; I could feel his eyes on me.

About thirty guests, holding drinks, mostly couples, made conversation in the open spaces of downstairs. I didn't see Charlotte. Alan pointed out the bar and left me to get myself a glass of wine. I found an Australian chardonnay among a regiment of spirits and poured myself a glass. Alan reappeared and led me across the room to where two women were talking by the fireplace.

"This is Jill Cummings," he said, making introductions. "Jill, Jason Walker."

Jill, a redhead with round blue eyes, looked at me with an appraisal of qualified interest. She gave me a thin, restrained smile and extended a white freckled hand. Alan stepped back slightly, placing his hand on the small of Jill's back in a gesture of subtle social courtesy, and, turning to the other woman, said, "And this is Penny Overfeldt."

"Pleased to meet you, Jason." Penny, a big-boned southern blonde with broad, strong shoulders and the tanned, square face of an athlete, extended her hand. She wore a giant diamond ring. Alan told them I was new to the island and walked off, leaving the three of us to get acquainted. These were seasonal regulars.

Penny's eyes moved from Alan's retreating figure to me. "How do you know Alan?"

"I don't, really."

"Then you're a friend of Charlotte's?"

"I saw Charlotte on the beach and we realized we'd met once

at a party in New York. I'm an acquaintance once removed, I suppose."

"Do you live in New York?" Jill asked. Her skin had an enameled whiteness that made her red hair striking.

"Until recently, on the Upper West Side near Central Park."

"I lived in New York for three years after college and I loved it. I was never bored."

"If you're bored in New York it's not the city's fault," I said.

"That's the problem of being from Atlanta. If you don't golf or watch football you can't talk to men. Talk about boring," Penny said. "But New York has a lot of gay men and *that's* boring. Then there's the overly sensitive type. I met a man recently who began to tell me about *his inner child!* I told him, 'Honey, people don't want to know about your little inner whatever.'" Penny began to laugh at her own comment.

The room was freshly painted and the hardwood floors shone with new polish. Vertical windows from the floor to the ceiling gave the room a special grandeur, and the late sun put golden light on the faces gathered there. An older woman with rheumy eyes and a somewhat forward manner that age sometimes takes as its right invaded our circle and introduced herself.

"I'm Sally Gross," she declared, with a look of appraising scrutiny. "Charlotte told me she'd met an interesting man at the beach, and that Alan had ruined everything."

Her candor made me chuckle. She leaned into me confidentially. "Being frank about Alan is our way of expressing sympathy for Charlotte. He's a little strange. He doesn't touch money, you know, because it's filthy."

"Really," I said.

"His is, or so I'm told."

Sally's amusing comment intrigued me. I'd heard Alan was involved with money laundering, never far removed from the drug trade; the pornography interest Madeline had told me about was an open secret. I looked around for him. He was on the other side of the room, offering a glass of wine to a woman in a white dress. I drifted in his direction. He was talking to two men about tax avoidance, a subject that clearly excited him. I was close enough to hear.

Alan's eyes shined with private intense glee as he spoke. "They don't have a right to force you. If you withdraw from the Social Security system—"

I recognized the argument, a crackpot rationale that taxation is illegal; I'd heard it before; it was the rant of born-again capitalists and borderline paranoids.

"Well, Alan," one of the men said, "you show us how it's done, and if you don't land in jail then you've converted us all."

He was still outlining avoidance strategies as he led them upstairs to show off his gun collection.

"Captain Walker," a voice from behind me said. I wasn't used to hearing myself called Captain. I turned and a man was smiling at me. "I'm Bill Schaffer," he said.

"How are you, Bill?" We shook hands. "Call me Jason."

He turned his head and made a sweep of the company, pointing out his wife across the room. "My wife, Emily, and I would like to charter your flying boat for an afternoon. Is that possible?"

"Sure."

"She thought a picnic would be great fun."

"I guarantee it will be memorable."

"We enjoy watching you take off and land. We thought what better thing to do than fly to an island beach for a day?"

"Absolutely. Here's my card."

"I'll call this number then." He put the card in his pocket. "Do you know the Lansings from St. Croix or New York?" he asked.

"We met in New York originally."

"Alan and I play golf together," he said. "Why don't you join us sometime?"

"I don't play. But thanks."

We shook hands and I moved away, drifting into a circle behind me where a Latin woman was deconstructing American vulgarisms: "Your language betrays your fears. Your enemy is not a swine as in other countries; rather, *he is one who has sex with his mother or himself!* You fear desire and so invent perverse expressions to vent your anxiety."

She's right, I thought; our defamations conjure impossible sodomies. "Fuck you, you fuck," for example, balancing the declarative with the pejorative, pretending invective for life's greatest pleasure. I was wondering about the subliminal implications of this when I saw Mitch Holden coming my way with Mrs. Schaffer at his side. They looked like a golden couple, Mitch tall and rugged, Emily Schaffer projecting health and energy. Her husband made a less overtly physical impression.

"We meet in all the right places, mate," Mitch said. We shook hands. "Have you met Emily Schaffer?"

"Your husband pointed you out to me. Pleased to meet you."

"Bill told me we're going to charter your Albatross for a picnic." Emily's blue eyes were wide as a child's. "I can't wait to ride in it."

Mitch said, "Emily was telling me how men and women favor different forms of suicide, did you know that?"

"Men favor firearms," Emily said, "or jumping from buildings; women favor drowning or poisons."

"Is that true?" My mind made a quick inventory of notable suicides. She watched me thinking.

"Women never play Russian roulette," said Mitch, quoting her.

"What conclusions do you draw?" I said.

"That men are inclined to make a mess, no matter what," said Emily.

"Also, men are needy," I said. "The extravagant gesture is always a form of 'Mommy, look!'"

"I think you're exactly right," Emily said. "And the aggressive satisfaction that someone else will have to clean up after them. It's petulance, after all, isn't it, a morbid strain."

Emily had something voracious in her comprehension, and definite charm. Mitch had the same sort of unusual nature. Whenever I sense a deeper understanding of someone, I begin to question what it is in myself I am seeing. Later, Mitch told me a little more about her. She was born in Barcelona, Spain, but moved to Argentina with her father after her mother died in an automobile accident. Emily was schooled in America. Strong, independent, decisive, intelligent, fearless: these were my impressions of her as I watched her move through the party.

I stood in the corner by the bar. The sun roiled on the wall and the room turned red. Moving into abstraction, I had a sudden impression of the inner life as a system of prisms, mirrors, and spheres, always in motion, only barely coherent. Late sunlight shone on the faces of these people around me, strangers with whom I shared that insoluble bond of our being alive together in the moment.

Charlotte approached; she was wearing a long earthen-colored cotton shift with red and green beads sewn into it in curious curving filigrees.

"I'm glad you came," she said, after kissing me on the cheek.

A woman at her side was in her late seventies or eighties, with pale white makeup, a white silk dress, purple lips, and an elaborate hat. She carried herself with fragile poise.

"This is Jasmine Richardson," Charlotte said, introducing us. "Jas is a local artist who has lived on the island for many years."

"Jason Walker," I said. "I'm pleased to meet you, Ms. Richardson."

"Please call me Jas. Charlotte was telling me you came here from New York to work on a book."

"I came here to establish a new life."

"And she told me that you fly the airboat we see land in the harbor."

"I do."

"I'm old enough to remember the Pan Am Clipper. It flew from New York to Lisbon before the war. I guess I should say World War Two; there have been so many since." She shrugged. "But I'm most interested in your writing. I've known some writers in my time and I've always admired their sense of quest. What quest does your work represent?"

"Petty vanity and lurid desire, I'm afraid; they're what I'm familiar with."

"You're not alone, my friend. We are all petty and lurid in our secret souls," Jas laughed. "Not everyone is honest about it."

I noticed Alan studying me from across the room; I seemed to be an object of special interest. The dissipating state of his marriage was on his mind. Antipathy expressed as frozen geniality was never my cup of tea.

The sun set and a dinner buffet was served.

I was looking out at the moon rising when Charlotte caught my elbow and squeezed it with the slightest pressure. "I want to tell you something." She walked me to the corner, out of earshot of the company. "I'm going to New York on Friday," she whispered.

"Next weekend? I'm going up, too."

"I know. I thought we could meet and go someplace together for a few days."

Thinking of the Beechcraft, I said, "I have a plane at a small airport about an hour north of the city. We'll fly away to some romantic place."

"Do you mean it?" Her smile was radiant.

"No," I said, examining my fingernails, "I always make extravagant promises I can't possibly keep because I want people to like me."

She punched my arm. "I'll call you tomorrow."

I didn't speak with her again that night except to say goodbye. On the walk home, silent and alone, I felt a sudden premonition, as if something was waiting for me in that house.

twenty-three

Mitch pointed to a good-looking ship at anchor about a hundred yards out, broad beamed but sleek. "Over there, *Threshold*. The fifty-eight-foot ketch." I could see it. "I've had her refitted. A Raymarine GPS with world maps and tide tables takes the guesswork out of entering harbors and channels: the entire world is digitally stored in its memory. She's got a satcom and fax for uplinking weather, and a navigation system below duplicated in the pilothouse. And an autopilot, of course."

"Planning a trip?"

He laughed. "I'm always planning a trip, mate."

"You told me you were a journalist on vacation. You didn't sail *Threshold* from Brisbane on a two-week holiday."

"I left Australia three years ago. I sail to a destination and moor the boat, fly back to work awhile, then return and sail someplace else. It's a different sort of life."

An accomplished sailor, Mitch had crossed the Atlantic and the Pacific alone. When I asked him about it he smiled at my innocence, at the impossibility of conveying the experience, but he spoke earnestly nonetheless. "It's half like living in a dream; the sea is always changing and your senses are keen to what's happening and about to happen. You learn to be alert in fatigue, no matter your exhaustion; the ocean never tires; it taunts you, but it rewards fortitude with visions, with insights. You'll never know sunrise except as the sun rises on the sea after a night of storm; or the moon until you've seen it shine on ocean waters a thousand miles from land; or enchantments of land and simple society until you've spent a month alone at sea. It's life away from distractions; miracles are a daily occurrence; you become attentive to the world's vibrations, what we disregard routinely in life on land. Then a day comes when the metaphor dissolves and there is no distinction between within and without, none, only clarity. It's something like what long-distance runners experience; all at once you're in a different zone, a place of enlightenment that makes you laugh like a raving maniac when you see it."

"And what is it that becomes clear?"

He put his finger to my temple. "A simple truth: the world is you, period. You thought it was something else: stuff, oceans and stars and rocks, but it will always be only you." He paused, examining his bottle of beer minutely. "The better part of me will always belong to the sea."

"Look who's holding up the bar." Charlotte was behind us. Mitch moved down a seat so she would be between us.

"Did you enjoy the party?" she said to Mitch.

"Very much."

"Emily Schaffer is meeting me here. Her husband is golfing with Alan." She turned to Mitch. "You met Emily at the party."

"I did. A charming creature," he said.

"They've chartered the Clipper for an afternoon," I said. "We're going to picnic on Peter Island off Tortola."

Mitch approved. "Little Harbor is a choice anchorage. Very quiet."

"They can fish or snorkel, whatever they want."

"Emily will love that."

"Excuse me a moment," Mitch said, leaving us for the Gents.

I put my hand on Charlotte's leg discreetly. "Are you set for Saturday?"

"I'll be in New York by Friday afternoon. I'm going up to Larchmont. I've got your cell number. I'll call you as soon as I land."

"I made reservations at a nice place upstate. We'll fly up in my plane on Saturday. I'll pick you up in the morning."

"I can't wait."

"I'm going to discreetly disappear," I said. She nodded.

Mitch returned as Emily came in. I said hello and good-bye, leaving the three of them together, thinking as I walked along the boardwalk how attractive the two women were and how much Emily resembled Mitch in undefined ways.

twenty-four

I felt different in New York this time; contentment made me immune to invidious comparisons, that subliminal disquiet that can't help pressing its nose to a certainty that in a city of 8 million tens of thousands are having a fuller life than yours, a life of promises kept, expectations met, dreams realized.

Charlotte appeared at the front door of her Larchmont home like a debutante standing in her dream. It was a large white colonial built before World War One, with the north shore of Long Island visible across the Sound beyond thick hedges in the backyard.

I tossed her bag into the back of my old Jaguar as she locked her house. She got in, leaned across the seat, and we kissed like honeymooners.

"You again," I said.

"Yes," she said, "it's me." She curled against me like a Cheshire cat. I felt a special kinship with Charlotte, as though we might discover that we were cousins, or that we had known each other as children.

We drove north on back roads along the Connecticut–New York border, where horse farms hover on sunlit ridges and restored barnyards are relics of an earlier era. The road rose and fell. Shadows flickered as we moved past trees in the bright sun. On the north end of a large lake I turned right at a road marked with a stone milepost and left at a gravel trail that led to an unmarked entrance to the airfield where I kept the Twin Beech 18. Unpretentious as a sheep meadow, its wide grass runway was concealed between two wooded hills. The air had that fresh country scent of damp earth, vegetable decay, and wildflowers. We drove through the gate and down the narrow path that ran the length of the runway. A cloud's shadow moved swiftly across the green grass, turning it blue. I drove slowly down behind the line of mostly older airplanes, perhaps ten in all. I stopped in front of my Beech 18, large and silver and gleaming, its two round engines distinctive, a thing of the air with the pedigree of something elegant from the road.

"That's *your airplane?*" she said.

"In all her glory."

"It's gorgeous!"

We got out of the car and I opened the aft entry. Charlotte leaned her head into the cabin and looked forward. Flying for the joy of it doesn't occur to most people until they're afforded the opportunity. Airplanes excite a romantic notion. Mine was done like a yacht. Curtains and wooden slatted blinds on the windows gave the cabin warmth; a cornice ran the length of the fuselage on both sides and there was a teak porthole at the rear. Four leather seats faced each other in the forward cabin, allowing enough room in back for two to sleep side by side.

"I carry an air mattress and all necessary camping gear. If it rains, you can seal yourself in and live quite comfortably."

"It's like a yacht."

"It is a yacht. An air yacht. I've been back and forth across the country a few times, up to Alaska, through the Bahamas."

"What incredible freedom." Charlotte was charmed, as I had hoped she would be.

We put our bags on board and I moved the car, parking it at the edge of the woods. Then I performed the usual exterior inspection, checking the fuel and oil for quantity and contaminants, pulling the props through, examining the flight controls for movement and integrity. When I climbed back in through the rear entry Charlotte was waiting for me, naked as a prom queen. "You better make sure *everything* works properly," she said. I was in front of her on my knees with a swiftness that should frighten pride.

Afterward, Charlotte got into the co-pilot's seat and studied the confusing array of switches, dials, and levers that looked to the unschooled eye like some monstrously complicated watchworks.

"Put this on," I said, handing her a headset.

When she had it adjusted, I switched on the battery master and spoke into the microphone: "How do you hear?"

"Loud and clear," she said.

"Ready?"

She nodded.

I started the engines and while the oil warmed I checked the radios and reset the gyros. Charlotte was absorbed with the experience. I moved the throttles slightly forward, and the plane began to move. I taxied to the north end of the runway and turned the plane around for the takeoff run.

On cool clear evenings in June, with the sun bright but lowering in the sky, the earth seems varnished in a golden hue. Sunlight fell on a hill just south of the field, making the western face of it bright. The hill is high and directly ahead, but you make a turn to the left after liftoff to avoid it. When I finished running the pretakeoff checks, I locked the tail wheel and scanned the runway to be sure it was clear.

"Ready?"

Charlotte nodded. I moved the throttles up; the engines went to full power and we began to roll across the grass. The land is slightly undulant, and you guide the airplane with gentle control over the contours, taking care not to be launched into the air too soon. At flying speed I eased the yoke back and the ground dropped away, then the landing gear went up; I banked left and the hill flashed past us.

The horizon got wider as we gained altitude. I flew north; we climbed between the white clouds floating in deep clear blue skies of early summer. Charlotte took my hand and squeezed it. We sailed over storybook estates, over dairy farms and waterfalls and apple orchards and wide uneven fields, over landscapes of epic beauty where the Hudson Valley has that quality of light you see in the paintings of Thomas Cole. I had forgotten the freedom flying low over hill country gives to the spirit, that Gnostic sense of being closer to *Good*, a means by which we comprehend how, as Emerson wrote, "dream delivers us to dream and there is no end to illusion."

We landed at an airstrip five miles from the Hudson Inn. The Hudson Inn is a country retreat famous for its gardens, its Olympian views, and its silence. I'd discovered it during weekend explorations away from the city. The inn itself was a former Dutch farmhouse. Once it had been a Trappist monastery; monastic reverence for visions informed its landscaping; its topiary hedges, hollows, and sudden spaces of private sunshine implied sacredness. Beyond a stone wall where the property dropped off, the Hudson River was visible; it shined like a silver band, shimmering through the hills with molten brilliance.

I called a taxi from the cockpit. It was nearing sunset. I secured the plane while Charlotte wandered to the edge of the woods to pick flowers.

In a short while the cab arrived. The driver, a young heavyset man wearing a blue baseball cap, helped us with our bags. "Beautiful night," he said, looking up. The clouds were bigger now and turning red in the west.

We drove across the field to where the road ran parallel, and Charlotte took my hand in the backseat. The trees were bright on the hills as we went along, and the houses very bright facing the sun, which at that hour cast shadows very long on the grass and dramatically dark.

Driving up, you could see that the main part of the inn was a half-timbered mansion with an oversize verandah that looked across the lawn into the woods. Tables were arranged for dining on the verandah. I had reserved a suite adjacent to the main building with a private entrance in back. The living room had a fireplace with a large mirror above the mantle, and the bedroom had its own door, going outside. We checked in while the driver dropped our bags at the suite, then went to dinner before the sun set.

A waiter in a starched uniform greeted us at the door to the dining room and led us to our table. I ordered a bottle of pinot noir; after the wine came we began to absorb our new surroundings in a relaxed frame of mind. We were unused to being together publicly. Her social reserve was gone now, replaced by a more animated girlish excitement.

"This is wonderful, Jason, really; it really is. The flight up was—there are no words for it."

"I'm glad you appreciate it. There is a timeless feel to this place, a peaceful remoteness."

"I love how you appreciate things, how you're not average, how you're not afraid of anything." Her eyes had the light of late day glowing in them.

"I'm afraid of a lot of things."

Charlotte's elbow rested on the table and her head was balanced rather elegantly on the thumb of her right hand. "How old were you when you learned to fly?"

"Fifteen."

"What got you interested?"

"My father was a pilot and there were pictures of airplanes in the house; he and his stepsister, my aunt, both flew; she became an air-show pilot; she took me up and did stunts when I was a kid. Learning to fly seemed like something done in the natural course of things, like riding a bicycle or driving a car."

"Do you like to sail? I've heard that pilots make good sailors."

"When I was younger I liked it a lot. What about you?"

"I've enjoyed it when I've gone with other people. I'm not a sailor, but I've lived near the water most of my life."

"I owned a sloop for a few years after college. Sailing's fine; it's just that flying has a keener thrill for me."

"You're a thrill seeker."

"Aren't you?"

We sat in the night air and the evening moved through us. The main course arrived with a bottle of Bordeaux. After the sun set and dusk faded, fireflies animated the darkness with flashes of yellow light. The conversation ranged over subjects we never touched on before, details that filled in a picture already drawn in bold strokes.

"What was your maiden name?"

"Givens. Clair Charlotte Givens. Clair was my mother's name."

"An honest, clean sound to it."

"My father called me Charlotte, but I like Clair, too. What's your middle name?"

"Thomas, and they called me Double-T in the Air Force."

"Double-T?"

"Every pilot has a call sign."

She thought for a moment. "Double-T: Terrible Trouble?"

"I like that," I laughed. "The truth is less dashing. When the Captain asked for my whole name on the first day in class I stuttered; I said, 'Jason T-Thomas Walker.' My ruthless classmates thought that was funny, so from that moment on they called me Double-T."

"But you are terrible trouble."

A woman knows what to say when she wants a man; flattery is her charm; it makes her radiant because we believe all of it.

"We seem to get along easily," she said. "I'm never bored with you. Most people are boring and difficult. Then I worry that it's me."

"I wouldn't worry."

"It shouldn't be so hard to have a happy life."

"My aunt Madeline once told me that happiness was the exclusive province of the lucky or the stupid."

"She said that?" Charlotte chuckled.

"I thought she was being funny."

"Which are we?"

"We've been both, I think."

"I'd like to meet your aunt."

"You have a lot in common."

"Jason, do you love yourself?" Her question, an abrupt shift, put me off balance. I couldn't answer it directly, which was revealing.

"I'm comfortable in my own company."

She laughed. "Do you feel like we're strangers to each other?"

"No, I don't."

"Rapport is a miracle, don't you think, the way we can see into the soul of someone else?" Her face had an inquiring aspect.

"Not everyone has that capacity," I said.

"Do you know who I really like, someone I've met recently?"

"Who?"

"Emily Schaffer."

"I liked her, too. But she's not easy to read. I wouldn't put her together with her husband; he doesn't have her edge."

"That was my impression, too. He seems innately intelligent but emotionally naïve."

"Isn't that what all women think about men?"

Charlotte laughed.

"I'm taking them to Peter Island next week for the afternoon."

"When the dust settles in my life, I'd love to go with you on a trip like that."

"We'll stay a week on the water."

Charlotte looked content. Talk about the future made her feel energetic. "Jason, I'm getting my life back again. I've been lost for so long."

"Maybe we met to help each other into the life we should have."

"I hope so."

We left the restaurant. I took her hand and we walked silently down the steps of the verandah to the pebble path that led to our suite.

On our first full night together free of interruption we slept fitfully; I'd awaken and her hand was resting affectionately on my shoulder, or her face was close to mine, or I was holding her at the waist, or turned away from her, my hand pressing her leg in a way to assure myself that she was there, and other such intimacies one after another that gave comfort and foreshadowed what being together might mean.

In the morning, Charlotte lifted her head from the pillow and pulled the curtain aside. The sky was vivid and cloudless. Bright summer sun shone through the trees in scattershot circles of light that lay like phantom gold on the green lawn. She threw the covers off, slid her legs over the side of the bed to get up, but my hand seized her arm and she brought her legs back under the sheets.

Later, she was making coffee in the small kitchenette. I was in the living room. The windows were thrown open to the sunshine. It was a morning of all possibility and every prospect of joy. We discussed venue; hiking was proposed and vetoed; bicycles were mentioned: "I'm lazy," I said.

Charlotte's head appeared in the doorway. "Then how about a picnic? The grounds are beautiful. We've got some wine. I'll make sandwiches."

A picnic was the perfect idea. When we finished preparations I sat on the porch in a giant garden grotto chair of gnarly lilac root, reading while Charlotte dressed.

"Are you almost ready?" I said when I had finished my chapter. "Almost."

I read another chapter, and another, and after many more minutes I went to look for her. I found her in the bathroom brushing her hair. I made a joke about women and time. Our heads came together in the mirror; we were both smiling, and our eyes met with that searching look that wonders how long anything good can last.

twenty-five

On a rock ledge a thousand feet above the Hudson River, at a place where Indians came to worship the moon, Charlotte and I spread our picnic blanket in bright sunshine. The scent of grass and warm earth enveloped us.

"Everything seems important now," she said. "I don't want to waste a second of life." Charlotte looked thoughtfully at the river below us; her face registered a complicated emotion. "I came close to death once."

"How?"

"Alan put something into my drink one evening. I was taken to the hospital."

I was continually shocked by new stories of Alan's bad behavior.

"He wanted to humiliate me."

"It sounds like he wanted to kill you. That's a felony, by the way; you're not allowed to poison people."

We talked more about her life with Alan and I had the same impression of a man with the phony charm of a cheap crook, a sociopath stranded in gloom.

"But why have you stayed with him?"

"I was ready to leave at least three times."

"What happened?"

"He threatened me; I felt vulnerable." She paused on that comment and the train of her thoughts seemed to shift. "Do you remember reading about the King Corporation?"

"Yes, I do. A business was acquired, stripped of its assets, and taken into receivership. There was a government investigation. Was that Alan?"

"He turned in the other officers, which was a travesty since he authored the scheme. He avoided jail, but it was a turning point. He was never the same."

"How so?"

"For one thing, he stopped touching money."

"Someone told me that at the party. It's very neurotic, you know."

"There was a period when he was normal. Sometimes I still see the wholesome Alan, the way you can see a youthful person through wrinkles of old age."

"What happened?"

"His dreams came true." She looked at me, then turned to the view. "They were bad dreams."

"Did he ever tell you what he was up to?"

"He's secretive about his business, but when things went wrong he blamed everyone, including me, for everything he hated about himself."

"But you saw through him."

"I pitied him. Emotionally I felt trapped. And when I started investing my own money he hated it."

Charlotte told me how her knack for investing annoyed him and how he insisted her success was beginner's luck, as though doubling, then trebling her portfolio was a simple trick.

"The funny thing was he was losing money at the time." She mused satirically: "My portfolio grew. I traded each morning, following fifty companies, shorting some, going long on others, mixing baskets, trading through three brokerage firms because each firm's research carried a different spin. I was disciplined, smart, aggressive, and I had luck. He couldn't stand it. He's competitive and hates to lose." Charlotte laughed, shaking her head at the ghost of a faded incredulity.

She looked at me. "I loved him once, or some idea of him, his charm, his promise. But he turned into someone empty. It surprised him that wealth didn't change much; he can't feel alive unless someone else is feeling pain. Hurting me was his way to feel something."

"You know how sick that is. Sick and dangerous."

"Well, that's what happened. One night when we were having an argument, and maybe liquor was talking, I told him, 'You're at war with yourself, Alan, and I don't know why. You attribute your anger to others, and I don't know why. You've demonized me, imagined me into something I'm not, and I don't know why.'

" 'You're wrong.' He glowered at me.

"I squinted at him. 'All your accusations are autobiography.'

" 'This is going nowhere.'

" 'You're right, Alan; nowhere is everywhere now; I'm absent and you're invisible; corpses are having this conversation.'

"I was speaking my mind with uncharacteristic frankness. I didn't know he'd put several crushed Nembutals into my drink. In a short time I became unsteady, slurring my words.

" 'You've been drinking a lot lately, have I mentioned it?' he said.

"I turned away from him and looked out the window where lights of other houses were visible on the shore. I didn't know what he had up his sleeve. In the kitchen, out of sight, out of earshot, he picked up the telephone and dialed nine-one-one.

" 'Yes, this is Mr. Alan Lansing, in Larchmont. . . . Yes. My wife has been drinking and she may have taken some drugs. . . . I'm not sure. She's incoherent; I'm worried. I think she needs to be hospitalized. . . . That's right. . . . All right. I'll be waiting.' By then I was asleep in the chair."

As Charlotte told me this story, I imagined Alan watching her while he waited for the medics, thinking with a smile how surprised she'd be when she woke, unable to recall the evening, the arrival of the ambulance, his explanations and apologies to the attendants. He would graciously accept their sympathy, their acknowledgment that he had done precisely the right and responsible thing in calling them. She regained consciousness in the hospital as they pumped her stomach, head throbbing in pain.

Charlotte leaned back and turned her head slightly to the side, looking at me in a way that gave emphasis to her words. "Do you know what it's like to wake up miserable every morning with a horror that tomorrow will be like yesterday, and today won't be different from a thousand identical mornings?"

"When did this happen?"

"The summer before we met at the New Year's Eve party."

I could not have known by her composed and radiant looks that Alan had been threatening her.

"I had no idea," I said.

"I must have seemed a little strange to you that night, I came on so fast."

"I wasn't complaining."

"It was out of character. You were handsome and seemed kind; I was desperate; I didn't know what to do."

The sun was high and strong, making the ground bright and hot. We moved our blanket to the cool shadows under a cluster of hemlock trees. Charlotte opened the picnic basket and took out the red gingham spread, the plates and knives and forks packed neatly there, and sandwiches we'd made, and a bottle of white wine, arranging it all. The wine looked gold against the green grass in the sun. She poured a glass for me and one for herself, and then we lay back, talking. We could see a sailboat on the wide part of the river far below.

"This isn't troubling for you to hear, is it?"

"I want to know everything you care to tell me. Did you consider leaving him?"

"I planned to. Then I got pregnant."

"Pregnant?"

"I miscarried."

"I'm sorry."

"The pregnancy never existed for him except as something I was doing to hurt him," she said.

"Alan's hostile by nature, isn't he?"

"Yes."

"I hear his gun collection is impressive."

Charlotte's laugh was a brief sardonic huff. "It's the pleasure of his life to fondle firearms."

Charlotte turned her head to the view. She took a hair from the top of her glass and sipped her wine. In the far distance, the sloop we had seen was coming about. The genoa fluttered as the bow crossed the wind line like a toy sail on a tiny toy boat.

"How far along were you in the pregnancy?"

"Five months. We were arguing. I fell."

"You fell?"

Now she turned in a way so that sunlight on the side of her face gave it a glow, and I thought how beauty brings no immunity from pain. She spoke in a slow, deliberate manner that seemed to let one vivid thought out at a time when many wanted to escape.

"We were having a fight upstairs. The fighting escalated. With all the shouting it didn't feel like my life, but like a drear day-dream someone else was having about hateful people."

She described the chase from the bathroom to the bedroom, from the bedroom to the hall, then to the stairs, a whirlwind of movement, and, "I fell backward. I could see his face get smaller and smaller, and the room tumbled, and that's all I remember. I woke in the hospital. They told me I'd lost the baby, a boy.

"Afterward I was too devastated to make a change; does that make any sense? Alan was penitent and tried to make it up to me. I thought he was sincere. We put masks on again. But after a while he became spiteful, peevish, and demanding at home, tape-recording telephone calls, refusing to handle coins or cir-culated bills: he disappeared into his symptoms."

Charlotte wanted me to understand something about her re-lationship with Alan that she barely understood herself. I thought how impossible it is to look at someone and know what their tragedies have been.

"I should have left him after I lost the first child. It was a mis-take to stay."

"You said 'first' child. There was a second?"

The question surprised her into hesitation; she waited a long interval before answering. "Yes. But I've said enough; I don't want to talk about that now."

I was happy that Charlotte had confided in me, though her reasons for not leaving Alan then were unclear. She poured an-other glass of wine and I leaned over and kissed her gently. We spent the day this way, eating, talking, strolling, drinking wine, and making love.

At dusk, we found another lookout high above the valley. The low sun drew a golden line across the mountains on the other side. For a while their tops shone, then they lost their color, but soon the moon rose and in its pale illumination everything changed again; the mountains seemed unreal, like something faintly remembered; we sat on the lookout watching the lights of villages below on the river. When the stars came out I pointed to Mars and showed Charlotte how to find Polaris; she put her head on my shoulder and we gave ourselves up to that communion when the world feels like a spiritual place and its mysteries are felt as the soul.

twenty-six

Living well is a habit of life. Back in St. Croix I woke early and watched the sun shine on the hills and on the hulls of boats in the harbor as I had my coffee. Then I went for a swim in the cove at the foot of the hill. The beach there was empty. The water is always warm and clear in the shallows, good snorkeling; I could see schools of fish in vertical formations, yellow ones with black stripes and blue ones that shone. I lost myself in their universe for an hour.

Afterward I lay in the sun for a while, then left the beach, went home to shower, and read by the window in my robe. When it was time to leave, I dressed in the blue shorts and white shirt that approximated a uniform for us, took up my knapsack, and walked to Christiansted, down King Street to the boardwalk, past the Comanche, RumRunners, Stixx, and the Chop House to our ramp. When I got to the plane, Johnny Buehn was standing at the landing gear wheel well draining the fuel sumps. We were flying cargo to San Juan.

"Looks good on the inside," he said. "I haven't checked the top yet."

The line crew normally serviced the plane with fuel and oil each evening after washing it, and each morning Johnny climbed on top of the wing to preflight.

I tossed my knapsack through the rear entrance. A breeze brought down the sweet fragrances of St. Croix: coconut, bread-fruit, hogplum, tan-tan, eucalyptus, plum rose, kumquat, and flamboyant. The sky was clear; a gentle wind rippled the water's surface offshore. The odor of dust and oil and vegetation rode on the salt smell of the sea; it was the good smell of island and airplanes and yachts.

The American Clipper appealed to the sort of passenger who favored unusual experience: airboat passengers rode in old-era luxury; they had room to walk around; they could dine on board or on the beach, sleep on bunks or in tents on overnights. There was a small library on board, and a bar. Dining could be as formal or informal as the clients chose, the table set on linen with silver, china, and crystal or a picnic. We tried to make it a memorable experience.

We flew cargo when we could; I enjoyed that; the schedule was flexible and cargo never complains. San Juan is a key mate-rials distribution station for the other islands. It's a short flight to Puerto Rico from St. Croix but a pretty one. We came in low over Culebra; the rolling hills rise up on the Puerto Rican coast; south, beyond the hills, the land gradient climbs sharply, be-coming sudden high mountains that disappear into blue dark clouds of the rain forest. We crossed the eastern shoreline on a direct course to Louis Muñoz Marin International, made a wide sweeping right-hand approach and landed on runway 10, and then taxied to the cargo bay. After leaving loading instructions, we took a cab into town for lunch.

The hotels and casinos along the north shoreline end at the bridge to Ilsa Grande. There is a small beach beside the bridge with shade trees and a pretty view of the bay. Not far from there is a small restaurant called *Hacienda*. French frame window shutters open to the ocean; tiled tables seem to hover above the surf. Bright yellow and green walls are painted in a mural of palm trees and cactus. It's a good place. Johnny and I went there for lunch.

After lunch we walked along Ashford Avenue where restored Art Deco buildings give the area distinction. The *Miami* stands out for its many-tiered apartments in peach, pale blue, and gray; the *Ashford Valencia* at number 876 has an eight-column portico and two white globe lights; farther along, there are bars and high-rise apartments and low single-story houses with locked fences and tiny yards by the bay on the other side. We had a good stroll, and when we got tired of walking we hailed a taxi back to the airport, where the Albatross was loaded and ready for the return flight.

It was four in the afternoon when we splashed down in the channel at Christiansted. Scattered showers were forming off the coast; we dodged them on our approach. Once up and turned around on the ramp, I shut down the engines. I stayed in the cockpit while the oil scavenge pumps ran; Johnny climbed up on top of the wing to check the fuel and oil as part of post-flight duties. When the scavenging was finished I switched off the battery and went outside. The line boys were standing under the wing. They spent two hours each night washing the exterior and the engines to clean off the salt.

I picked up my knapsack and waited for Johnny. He finished the checks, climbed down, and got his bicycle and I met him at the front of the airplane.

"We've got the Schaffer charter tomorrow. We'll need a mate.

I was going to ask Yarrow Thompson to come along. Think she'd be interested?"

"She'd love it."

"Is she over at the Comanche now?"

"I think she's at Stixx tonight," Johnny said. "Want me to come with you?"

"Not if you have something else to do. I'll tell her to meet you here at nine tomorrow and you can give her a shopping list."

"That'll be fine," Johnny said. "I'll see you in the morning."

Johnny rode off and I started home on foot along Watergut Street, the narrow road that runs along the waterfront. It ends where the boardwalk dock begins. Just past the first slip I heard my name called.

"Saw you land tonight, Cap'n. You just floated out of the clouds like some big fish come down from the moon." Old John Moses, a retired fisherman, went to the ramp each morning to watch the *Clipper* depart. Authentic Old Salt, he was always prowling the docks.

"How's business?" he asked.

"Staying afloat."

Old Moses twitched his head and laughed like a child every time I gave him the line. "Miami tomorrow?" he asked, throwing his head back with that old man's stiff interrogative flourish.

"Tomorrow we've got a charter. Johnny and I are taking a couple of people to Peter Island off Tortola. They want to fish and snorkel. I'm looking forward to it myself."

He shook his head with amusement. "You gonna fish off the wing?"

"I might just do that."

"Fish don't know where a hook come from, like as good from an airplane as a rock, I guess."

I laughed and said good-bye to Old Moses and continued on to Stixx in that happy mood that comes as a day of good work turns into a night with no commitments.

These days Yarrow never had a steady job, didn't want one, but she was always working and you saw her at a different place every night, covering shifts for absent bartenders or helping a manager out on a busy night. She crewed on sailing charters when the regular crew was off island or on vacation or sick; she painted houses and boats, did yard work for the town of Christiansted, even sold real estate. She was good with people, reliable, and she knew everybody, a perfect supernumerary for the charters we wanted to make a more significant part of the business. She put down a rum and Coke for me. Stixx was alive with regulars and tourists, a usual crowd for this time in the afternoon.

"How would you like to crew for Johnny and me on an air-boat charter tomorrow morning?"

"I'm flattered," she said. "I'd love to. What time?"

"We'll plan to take off at ten; if you show up at nine, that'll be fine. Johnny will have a list of things to get at the market. Plan for about five hours."

"I'll be there."

"Good."

"Is there anything special I should bring?"

"Just yourself and a bathing suit."

She leaned across the bar. "I've really wanted to fly with you guys. Thanks so much for thinking of me."

I was pleased. A good crew makes a difference. I was on my way out as Mitch Holden came in.

"Got time for a beer?" he said.

"Sure." It was a good night to drink. We sat down together.

"How've you been, mate?"

"Can't complain. Just flew in from San Juan. Tomorrow we've got a charter to Peter Island."

"Emily and Bill Schaffer."

"How did you know?"

"She told me."

"Where did you see her?"

"Shopping on King Street. She's looking forward to it. I know Peter Island. Little Harbor is where you want to go."

"That's exactly where we're going."

Yarrow said hi to Mitch and brought our beers and Mitch had a sip of his and his face frowned.

"How much do you know about Alan Lansing?" he said.

"Personally or professionally?"

"Both."

"Personally: he's got a lot of money; he's a prick. Professionally: he squeezed money out of a merger my partners and I were completing a year ago, a greenmail scam."

Mitch's expression grew serious. "He used to do some business with people I knew a few years ago, people with a certain reputation. He's a good person to steer clear of."

"He's got nothing I want."

"You're sleeping with his wife, mate."

"They're divorcing."

"He doesn't see it that way."

"What are you saying?"

"A few people I know heard him bring up your name in less than flattering terms. Also, an acquaintance of mine has offices near Lansing's on Company Street, same building. They keep the shutters open during the day. He overhead a conversation Lansing had with someone about the arrival of an important person who works for him. 'Tell him to fly to St. Thomas and charter the airboat. Jason Walker is the pilot to contact. I want to incorporate the airboat into the operation.' Then he heard the other guy say, 'Put the pilot on our payroll?' Lansing said, 'No, no, I'm just going to enjoy a game of chess,' whatever that meant."

"Thanks for the warning. I'll keep an eye out for some Mr. Big."

Mitch winked. His bottle touched mine.

I thought about who Alan Lansing might be expecting. His two sidelines were money laundering and pornography. If some big shot was arriving it should be easy to tell which world he came from. It sounded like drugs. These days product moved through Haiti across Hispaniola on interior roads to airfields in the Dominican Republic. From there it was put on boats or flown in small aircraft of all types, including helicopters and ultra-lights. It wasn't like the old days, when a Learjet could piggyback on some airliner's transponder, then drop back during the descent and land at a remote strip. Today's smuggling methods required many moving targets to create a porous front. The Albatross was ideal for this.

I knew Alan kept his distance from dirty work; he was Mr. Clean, who wouldn't touch legal tender. But he had his uses. The discreet disposition of vast quantities of cash was always a problem for successful dealers. They didn't have his offshore connections, nor could they fathom the complexity of transactions that moved money through an electronic labyrinth of dummy corporations. Alan did. The fees for such expertise were steep of course.

Alan loved capital synergies. Nothing offered faster legitimate profits than sex; in America, pornography grossed more in a year than all professional sports combined. Pornography was found money, clean money, and a business of low overhead and unlimited appeal. The rumor was he'd bought a production company in Canada, neatly funded by laundered revenues, the money sheltered in banks of island nations. It made sense.

Mitch implied a setup of some kind. Alan Lansing didn't frighten me. He was a bully, and a bully is always a coward. I was grateful to Mitch; by telling me what he'd heard he was being earnest on my behalf, putting me on watch, but it gave me that unsettled feeling of everybody knowing more about my business than I did.

twenty-seven

Next morning, I was standing under the wing when Yarrow Thompson drove up on her Vespa with a basket full of sandwiches and ice. "Johnny said they wanted basics."

"Let me help."

I took the bags out and we went aboard the Clipper to put the food and ice in the ice chest, then sat together in the forward cabin to talk about the trip. Johnny came out of the cockpit and handed me the Sectional Aeronautical Chart. I let Yarrow see the route we'd take.

"This is Peter Island," I said. "It's on the south side of Sir Francis Drake Channel across from Tortola. We'll land at Little Harbor on the northwest side and anchor in the shallows offshore."

"I've been there," Yarrow said. "It's a great place; you'll have twenty feet of depth, even at low tide."

"Good."

"What do you want me to do?"

"Get familiar with the lines and the anchor up front. The bow hatch opens in. You'll handle the mooring when we land."

Yarrow went forward. She was good with boats and I was glad to have her with us. I noticed, too, that she had the same general demeanor as Johnny, energetic, helpful, and direct; they seemed to work well together. A Jeep pulled up with our clients; I went aft to greet them as Johnny was finishing his preflight.

"The Schaffers are here," I said.

Bill Schaffer was a pleasant person, about my age, early forties, dressed in khaki slacks and a yellow shirt with a collar and Top-Siders. His eyes ran along the lines of the Albatross with the excitement of a child for his first bicycle. His wife, Emily, a few years younger, had that blond large-boned look of female Scandinavian athletes. She wore a white cotton frock over her bikini, and rubber flip-flops. Emily's eyes were light blue, intelligent, and, as Charlotte noted when we had talked about her, expressed a different, deeper, more circumspect character than her husband's. How quickly we size people up, I thought.

They took two large bags out of the back of the Jeep and began to walk over to the plane.

"Hand those to me," I said, standing at the rear entry. Bill Schaffer pitched his bag up, then I took Emily's, and Emily climbed in and then her husband behind her.

"What a beautiful airplane," she said, delighted. The interior brass fixtures, sconces, wooden venetian blinds over the portholes, sand-colored carpets, green leather seats, and shining mahogany bulkheads gave the cabin a feel of the great wooden boats of the thirties. "When was this airplane built?" she asked.

"Nineteen-fifty-one."

Bill Schaffer surveyed the airboat with a yachtsman's eye. "Are there many still flying?"

"Maybe forty in the world."

Johnny and Yarrow stepped through the cockpit hatch; we were all aboard in the cabin and ready to depart.

"This is Johnny Buehn, First Officer," I said, making introductions, "and Yarrow Thompson, your mate."

"Glad to meet you all."

"Let me give you the plan," I said. "We're going to fly northeast about sixty miles, to a small island with a good beach and a nice shelf of coral. We'll drop the anchor and inflate the Zodiac, and you can use the wing for a diving board, fish, do whatever you like; the coral is razor sharp, though, so when you're swimming be careful not to touch it. We've got sandwiches for lunch, a full bar, and ice, so whenever you're ready we'll get under way."

"Where shall we sit?" Emily asked.

"Anywhere you want."

I went up to the cockpit while Yarrow got them settled; they took their seats amidships by the bubble window where you can see forward along the side of the plane. Johnny pulled the ladder up and stowed it, closed the aft entry doors, then came up to join me at the controls.

Once the engines were started I cleared the area and nudged the throttles forward; the plane began to move; we went down the ramp and I did our checks as we drifted into the channel. When we were ready, I looked back to be sure all was well, then slowly pushed the throttles up. The engines whined and the plane began to accelerate. We went faster and the bow rose up over the waves. At flying speed we broke from the water; our shadow fell away but chased us like a ghost of our bondage to gravity.

I held the magnetic course until the island came into view as a thin line on the horizon, then dropped down to a hundred feet, and maneuvered to landing where the ocean calmed at the coral shoals.

We moved slowly through the narrow channel. Once in the lagoon, I sailed to the east end. Yarrow went forward through the catwalk to the bow compartment. She opened the hatch and prepared to drop the anchor. When I gave her a signal she tossed it forward. I put the props in reverse and the airboat backed up gently as she paid out sixty feet of scope. When the anchor was set she tugged hard to check for security. At her thumbs-up I shut down the engines. We were moored.

Little Harbor looked ideal. Steep green hills dropped to the shore. The sands were white and the water was green and aquamarine. I could see the bottom clearly; schools of yellow fish were swimming in dense vertical formations. Johnny took Emily and Bill Schaffer to shore in the Zodiac. Emily Schaffer waved. I waved back. Johnny motored back to pick us up and in a few minutes we were all together on the beach.

The Schaffers were easy clients. They swam, collecting shells; they sunned; Yarrow set a table under one of the trees and prepared a lunch of fresh salmon and cheese and baguettes and white wine for the Schaffers. We ate together, and afterward the five of us lay on the beach, talking, bathing, dozing, and letting time pass without a care.

We got acquainted. Emily told us she had spent her teenage years on a cattle ranch in Argentina. "My mother was Spanish," she said. "I grew up in Madrid. They sent me to school in America. But my father was a rancher and he wanted to live in Argentina. My mother agreed to the move but died in a motoring accident before we left Spain. I went with my father and stayed with him for three years, near Buenos Aires."

"What is Buenos Aires like?" I asked.

She made an effort to be candid the way people do when the subject is dear and they sincerely want you to know about it. "It has unexpected grandeur," she said, "like Paris or Rome, but different, as though the culture went sideways somehow. There is something wild below the surface: men and women tango in the afternoon; nights begin at ten o'clock; there is a love of beauty but also longing in the national character, they say because so many have come from other places." As she told it, I thought how apt a description of her it seemed.

Bill Schaffer, Johnny, and Yarrow went snorkeling. Emily and I walked the length of the beach, climbed a small hill, and explored the other side, where it was rocky and volcanic. Emily threw a rock into the water and watched the expanding ripples. Then she turned suddenly.

"This is a dream," she said, pointing to the flying boat drifting at anchor on the pale aquamarine shallows. She squinted into the view. "When I was a little girl, I wanted to go to faraway places and see exotic sights."

"Is this exotic enough?" I said.

She laughed.

"You remind me of Mitch Holden," I said. "The Australian. You know him. He's an exotic."

She looked at me with new curiosity, holding her hand above her eyebrows to block the sun. "Do you know Mitch well?"

"Well enough. He's an adventurer."

"I like that about him," she said, and then moved away from the subject. "What brought you to St. Croix, Jason?"

"I had an opportunity to fly the plane you see right there. Seemed like a good change."

"Has it been?"

"It's nothing like the life I had in New York. But I came here following my instincts, and I'm happy I did."

"Following instincts can be dangerous."

"Danger clarifies."

"It can also destroy."

"You've survived," I said, with a wry tone. She smiled at that: I had her wavelength.

When we got back to the other side Bill Schaffer was drying himself with a towel.

"Anything interesting on the other side?" he said.

"More of the same: sun, sand, and surf."

Emily took the towel and dried his back. Together the Schaffers had that contemporary aura of youth, prosperity, and health. He was boyishly handsome and educated to the money trades, a type I knew from New York: sensible, practical, genial, and good, yet in some nebulous overall sense clueless. Emily gave a different impression; she had something about her I couldn't quite reach; she radiated raw appeal; her lean body advertised fitness and sex, the female animal. She was bright, curious, and clandestine, with formidable qualities she failed to quite conceal. She had the look of someone who knows something about you that you don't know yourself. Women like Emily Schaffer come in two flavors: virtuous and dangerous to know.

Outwardly they seemed the perfect couple; he was a bright, inoffensive hale fellow of fortunate circumstances, but her eyes had that worldly understanding that life is partly always a show of success to conceal a truth of half-admitted failure.

After a while the sun was very hot and the beach sands were hot and we all went for a swim together. The Schaffers went snorkeling one more time and I took some pictures with a plastic camera. We started to prepare to leave the beach.

The Schaffers finished their bottle of wine in the shade while Johnny took Yarrow and me back to the airplane to get ready for our departure. When everybody was aboard, Yarrow went forward and weighed anchor. I started engines and taxied out. It had been a good day; every face was flushed with sunburn.

On the flight back to Christiansted, Emily sat facing forward in the club seats on the starboard side. Occasionally I turned around and caught her eye; some non-specific quality radiated from her that in a man is called cool; in a woman I don't know what you call it, but Emily was showing me she had it.

The wind had come up and takeoff was rougher than normal. When we got to Christiansted I circled the town, banking left over Protestant Key. Touchdown in the protected channel was smooth; after we were parked, Bill and Emily Schaffer couldn't say enough about the experience. All agreed the afternoon had been a great success. We said good-bye on the best of terms.

twenty-eight

Jason:

Falling in love is like building a fire. First, the materials have to be there, there has to be a spark, the spark has to make a flame, and the flame has to be carefully tended until it catches. Sometimes the flame goes out at the beginning; sometimes it flares up brightly but dies before it takes hold. But once it gets going for real, the fire grows hot and consuming and hard to put out. Hate has the same M. O.

Madeline

I had been working on the Corona Standard Portable at my small table when I heard sirens. Curious as anyone when the sirens got louder, I followed the others toward black smoke rising from an abandoned sugar plantation beyond the nearby hill. The manor house was on fire, its roof burning furiously as a brisk wind whipped the flames. The house was a fixture, one of those eccentric stone mansions from the last century with trees grown up around it. Firefighters moved in urgently, barking orders back and forth. I could feel the heat of flames from where I stood. We onlookers watched mesmerized as, perhaps from a single spark, the flames had grown into a monster of heat and destruction, visible, real, with the character of something from the spirit world. When the roof collapsed, sparks flew up from the fiery inside and there was a collective expression of awe. The firefighters moved closer in and everyone was at a high level of excitement. After a while, the firefighters began to close in and the monster retreated, leaving the building a smoking stone ruin.

You had to respect the primitive forces—that a candle flame could grow to conflagration. The omen found fertile ground in me; the theme of the moment became fire: fire's destruction, nature's indifferent devastations, seizures of violence that take hold of whole nations, bombs that drop, war, holocaust, lightning bolts that kill randomly, volcanic eruption, earthquake, all the apocalyptic hazards of this life, and imagined hellfire of damnation in the next. I started back to my apartment with a sober sense of vulnerability.

On the way I ran into Mitch Holden. He had seen the fire from his boat and, like me, he had been drawn by the spectacle; now he was walking back.

"Bloody awful," he said.

We walked together along the side of the road. The pebbles were hot from the sun, and the dry dust rose like smoke at each footstep.

"I'm headed back to town," Mitch said. "Want to have a drink?"

"Maybe later. I've got a quick flight to St. Thomas. By the way, I took Bill and Emily Schaffer on a charter yesterday to Peter Island."

"How did it go?"

"She loved the airboat."

"She would."

"Her husband's a nice guy. They both seemed to have a good time."

An abstracted smile formed on Mitch's rugged face. We said good-bye where the road went into town.

I met Johnny at the ramp and we took the *Clipper* to St. Thomas to pick up six passengers, two men and four women. The men were middle-aged, on a sybaritic vacation with the women. People come to the islands to relax. How they relax is their business.

"Good afternoon, Captain," the shorter, more intense man said. He had dark scrutinizing eyes and chestnut brown skin. "My name is Enrico DaSilva. This is my associate, Bernard Bonaventure."

"*My associate*" is a term that establishes the superiority of the person who uses it first.

"You came highly recommended," he continued, "and I understand you charter this magnificent ship. We would like to charter it for a day while we're on St. Croix."

"That won't be a problem," I said. I helped them aboard. The women were attractive in the Latin way of sexual dignity that wobbles on high heels and leaves a wake of cheap perfume. They pressed their noses to the portholes and the men enjoyed the comforts of the cabin, where wine and spirits were available from crystal carafes in the bar cabinet.

After we landed and ramped the Albatross, the man called Enrico made an appointment for a charter. "Is the day after tomorrow all right?"

"That will be fine." I handed him my card. "Call me tomorrow to confirm."

"We'll make a happy little party," he said, nodding to the women.

They left in a taxi and Johnny and I secured the *Clipper*. Johnny had begun to unroll the freshwater hose to wash down the plane.

"See if Yarrow can join us," I said.

"You mean it?"

"Sure. We need a mate."

"She'll be there, not to worry." Johnny had a look about him of the perennial boy, and any mention of Yarrow now put a big smile on his boyish face.

"You and Yarrow have a thing?"

"Seems that way."

"See you both tomorrow, then."

"Roger that."

I walked along the boardwalk and felt good about the day. That lasted until I stopped at the mailbox outside my apartment. There was a small packet with no return address. I opened it. It was a DVD, no markings, no note. I went upstairs and, after pouring a glass of wine, turned on my laptop and popped in the disk. The digital image was of Charlotte on her hands and knees, an agonized expression on her face, an agony of pleasure. She was out-of-doors. The camera moved. I recognized the cliff at the Hudson Inn where we'd had a picnic, and then I saw my own image. Someone had followed us and filmed us. Alan? It seemed impossible. I had flown my plane; no one could have followed us. Someone had traced my hotel reservation; someone was monitoring my computer. Shock turned into an angry sense of violation as I wondered what else was being watched.

twenty-nine

When you let someone into your life their problems become your problems. Charlotte was right: Alan Lansing had a different reference to reality; I didn't know if he was dangerous or just a freak, but Mitch seemed to think he was dangerous, and so did Madeline. I was sitting at the Comanche bar thinking about things.

The Comanche was as busy as I'd seen it all season. When you've been under surveillance it makes you suspicious of everyone. I looked at each person seated at the bar trying to comprehend something about the DVD. Alan might follow Charlotte and spy on her, but he wasn't the type to watch his wife betray him, not with me; he would have interrupted us. I felt certain that the film was made by a third party. If a private detective working for Alan made the film, sending me a copy was a try at intimidation. What was certain was that my computer had been monitored, because no one, not even Charlotte, knew where I planned to take her that day.

I ordered another drink. Reggae music played in the background; the sound of steel drums and voices blended into the din. Moonlight on the harbor made a silver lambency that silhouetted the boats, and the chime of halyards came off the water, adding live accents to the music.

I finished my drink and signaled the bartender. He handed me the tab; I paid it, left a good tip, and walked down the stairs to Strand Street.

The night air was warm under clear, starry skies. I decided to go down along the docks. I took a narrow alley off the main street. I walked carefully, mindful of potholes. The moon was nearly full and bright with blue light and I heard the brittle rattle of palm fronds in the sea breeze.

Before I saw anything, I felt someone watching me. A moment later a figure came out from the shadows. The figure facing me was standing to the side of the alley. He had a face like a hatchet and a barrel chest, with eyes like tiny olives. I moved back. A second figure stepped in front of my path; he was thin and tense. Then a third appeared who seemed to be the leader; three figures stood together as I approached. I thought to run, but they were close enough to catch me, and I wasn't sober anyway. I stopped short of them. They didn't say anything. For what seemed like a long interval no one moved.

"What's up with you guys?" I said.

"We got a job to do," one of them said.

"A job to do on you," another one said.

"Shut up," said the third.

The drinking had made me calm and their manner with one another seemed hapless. I could tell they were serious, though, and I was willing to give them whatever was left of my cash.

"I don't have a lot on me," I said.

"Shut up," the other said again, this time to me. His face appeared in the moonlight, angry, snarling, "Take him."

"What the—" The other two jumped me, pushing me to the ground, while the first stood as a lookout. I was overwhelmed, pinned down, and punched hard in the stomach. I couldn't breathe. When I stopped struggling they dragged me to my feet.

"Take him to the beach; we'll do him there."

The beach was fifty yards distant. The punches knocked the wind out of me; I had trouble walking and started to vomit. When I vomited, one of the guys let go of me. The full seriousness of what was happening awakened in me; I broke the other's hold and started running, putting all pain to the side.

"Motherfucker," one of them yelled. They came after me.

I ran as fast as I could, but I didn't get far; they caught me near where the boardwalk ends. I felt hands on me and then I was on the ground again. My fingers dug hard into the face of the one holding me down and he let go. I kicked out trying to get balance, twisted around, and felt a kick in the ribs as I tried to get up. I fell back and someone was on my legs. Above me I saw a knife blade flash in the moonlight. The knife came down; I rolled fast to the left and the blade missed my shoulder. I heard: "Cut his face." Then, as though from out of a dream, a voice I recognized called out; it was Mitch Holden running toward me screaming, "I'll kill you motherfuckers. . . ." The one with the knife turned and lashed out as Mitch hit him at full speed; he went down hard. Mitch's body was tense, his fists poised. I broke free, rolled over, and grabbed a piece of driftwood. I smashed the head of the hatchet-faced one who had kicked me in the ribs. He didn't go down, but he staggared back, hurt. Mitch kicked the knife out of the downed man's hands and it scuttled across the broken pavement. Mitch's eyes were purple with violence; he stood motionless as a coiled snake. The third man stayed back in the shadows, unsure what to do. Mitch threw his hands out and let out a fierce ululation, a war cry that could be heard across the harbor. The three men backed away, paused for a moment, and ran off, disappearing into the narrow alley again. I looked at Mitch. We were both breathing heavily. I threw down the driftwood club and leaned against a palm tree by the edge of the beach. Palm fronds above us rattled; clouds were strewn along the hills, and the sea was silver and shining in the Caribbean moonlight.

"Are you okay?" Mitch said. His eyes were calm now.

"I think so."

"They wanted to kill you, mate. Who were they?"

"I have no idea."

"What were they after?"

"I don't know. They jumped me."

The beating left me numb in the jaw, but I could feel pain in my ribs. The hatchet-faced guy had connected hard; there was some satisfaction to know he'd wake up with a headache.

"I was headed to the boat. I heard them yelling. It didn't sound right."

"I saw you get cut," I said. "Look at your shirt."

Mitch's shirt was sliced diagonally, but there was no blood. He smiled and took out a newspaper he had put against his chest for protection. "An old trick from randy days."

My breathing was steady and my head was clear. I put my hand on his shoulder. "I thought I was through with this sort of thing a long time ago."

"Let's find a taxi."

Mitch walked with me until we got to King Street near the fort where the taxis wait. When I got home, I went up the stairs to my apartment and, making sure the door was locked, got into bed.

I slept soundly. I woke in the morning with aches and pains, but nothing appeared broken. Someone had it in for me, that was certain, and I had a pretty good idea who it was.

thirty

I felt like a chump; Alan had marked me: this would not stop until I was dead. That wasn't an option. To begin with I had to unbug my computer and then get as much information on Alan Lansing as I could. I knew who to call.

Melrose Maynard was a boy wonder who had saved one of our big Internet deals. We had a software glitch somewhere in our search engine. It had to be chased down before the deal could close, and we were running out of time. I explained the problem to him. "This shouldn't have happened," I said.

"If couldn'ts and shouldn'ts were candies and nuts we'd all have a wonderful Christmas. Get me a suite at the Waldorf and a bottle of Johnnie Walker Black. Leave me alone for twenty-four hours."

My partners and I got him the suite and the bottle. We spent all night and the next day pacing like nervous husbands waiting for him to deliver. Sure enough, Melrose emerged with the new software, and I don't know what he did or how he did it, but he saved a multi-million-dollar deal from falling through. He's the best I've seen.

"Melrose, this is a private matter; you don't have to feel obligated," I told him.

He laughed. "You brought me into the big game, Jason; I'm happy to help."

"I need a few facts on a man named Alan Lansing. You may know the name. He's a venture capitalist. He worked for a firm called G&LJ a few years ago and tried to queer our merger."

"Vaguely familiar. I wasn't on the business end of things."

"I've heard he launders money. For who, I don't know. See what you can dig up. I want anything you can find on the guy: who he talks to, what he's into, how much he's got, and what he does with it."

"Where do you think the accounts are kept?"

"I'm not sure. I suspect offshore havens in the Caribbean, because he comes down here to vacation."

"A man likes to feel close to his cash."

"Precisely."

"Nevis is newly popular."

"One more thing. I got a DVD in the mail. A film of me and his wife in flagrante, as it were."

"Whoops."

"See if it's a got a signature somewhere on it."

"Roger dodger."

"Also, my computer was monitored; have you got something to fix it?"

"Purge your C-drive and I'll send you a super-duper firewall. Be sure you're starting fresh."

"Thanks, Melrose. I owe you one."

"No problemo."

thirty-one

"It is a beautiful airplane," Enrico DaSilva enthused as he boarded the *American Clipper* with his entourage for an afternoon of drinking and swimming at Peter Island. DaSilva was a short, intense man with dark hair and vivid black eyes. Mr. Bonaventure, whom Enrico called Bernard, was less intense and seemed to be enjoying the novelty of the charter immensely. They and their four lady friends made a cheerful party. Yarrow, Johnny, and I flew them out to our favorite place, Little Harbor.

When we were established on the beach, Enrico DeSilva's aspect changed from watchful wariness to aggressive lighthearted banter. "Bernard, come here; help us set up." Bernard put down a box of food and wine and went over to Enrico. Johnny and Yarrow set up a portable tent. Inside the tent we unfolded a double table with rattan chairs, linen, flowers, china, and silver, until it looked like an advertisement for Holland and Holland,

London. I carried four folding chairs from the Zodiac while two of the women, Beatrice, a dark-eyed Dominican beauty in a thong bikini, and Roberta, sexy with light skin and blue eyes, began to throw a plastic beach ball. They were younger than the other two women, who remained at the table, now configured with candelabra, where Enrico and Bernard were smoking cigars and sipping champagne. When everyone was settled, Johnny went to the other side of the beach to fish, which was his way of passing time on these charters; Yarrow stayed nearby to be certain that the clients had what they wanted. I sat in the sand thinking and watching the airplane, making sure it didn't drift at anchor. I enjoyed the sight of it floating quietly in the lagoon, above the yellow coral on the bright green water in the sun.

"Captain, would you care for a cigar?"

"No thank you."

Enrico held his cigar up to admire it. "These are Macanudos, but made with Dominican tobaccos, superior to Cuban Macanudos. The Cuban tobaccos have fallen in quality in the years of Castro's communism. Ours have only improved."

"The women also are the finest," said Bernard, watching the girls playing catch.

"Ours are the best women and the best cigars in the world," Enrico DaSilva agreed, smiling. "Truth is truth." Then he said something profane in Spanish about Cuban *puta* and Bernard laughed heartily.

"Don't tell Roberta or it will go badly for you later. Roberta is Cuban," Bernard said to me confidentially, and laughed. His mustache and large teeth made his grin seem wide and lascivious.

Enrico was enjoying himself. "Captain, how long have you had your airplane?"

"We've been operating here for five months."

"You have regular service to where?"

"St. Thomas, St. John, Tortola, and three times a week to San Juan."

"And charters?"

"Anywhere."

Enrico DaSilva gazed thoughtfully at the *Clipper*. "I'd like to charter your plane for some private business," he said candidly and directly.

"As long as it's legitimate," I told him.

He smiled, pursed his lips, studied the ash on his cigar, and then looked up. The girls had moved the game of catch into the water, punching the ball high into the air again and again.

"Look at the girls. They play like children."

"I want to swim," said one of the women at the table, a tall Latin blond in a yellow bikini whose name was Maria; she pulled Bernard Bonaventure's arm.

"No, Maria," Bernard Bonaventure said. "You go." He pushed her hand away.

"Ach, you are lazy to swim." She got up and sauntered to the surf with a show of sullen pique. Bernard laughed, looked at me, and shrugged.

Watching them enjoy the day, I wondered about that class of criminal willing to risk everything, personal freedom, even life itself, for a few years of high living. It was easy to know how a person like that could be dangerous. The smiles and banter and lewd jokes were not an expression of a sunny disposition.

I didn't have any illusions about Enrico DaSilva. Deep down inside I also feared they had not found me through serendipity.

thirty-two

I had come home after a day of flying and the letter was under my door. . . . *I lay in bed half-asleep, thinking of you, trying to make sense of my life. . . . I believe in the possibility of our sharing a life together with great happiness, and I will let nothing stand in the way of that happening as long as you give me an indication that this is also something in your heart. . . .* I was reading it for the fourth or fifth time when I heard knocking. I put the letter down and went to the narrow stairs. The door opened below and she was there.

"Charlotte!"

I was thrilled she had come but unprepared for what I saw as she came closer. Her face was swollen on the left side above the eye. The eye itself was red and her mouth was cut. I was shocked at her appearance.

"Sit down. What happened?"

"Alan. He lost it. He beat me. This is the last time."

"Have you called the police?"

"I don't want the police." She was adamant.

I led her to the chair by the window, and when she was seated I got her a glass of wine.

"What happened?"

"He went crazy, screaming at me, chasing me in the house, accusing me of all kinds of things. He's unhinged. He wants to kill you."

"I believe it."

"He was drunk last night and started rambling about some drug deal he's involved with. He told me he'd fixed it so you'd go to jail. Be careful, Jason; someone could plant something here or in the plane and you wouldn't know about it. Money buys him a lot of protection, believe me; I don't know what he's capable of."

Rage is stoic: I listened calmly to Charlotte. Before me was a woman whose face was beaten and raw, her eyes red and distended, with bruises on her forehead suffered at the hands of a man who was scheming to destroy both of us. And even then I did not yet know the full story. Charlotte had not found the forbearance to tell me.

She put her hands to her face and began to sob and her expression dissolved as twelve years of argument, abuse, lies, innuendo, and subterfuge flooded out. I tried to fathom Alan while I held her hand. When she calmed down I poured her another glass of wine.

"There was a reason I stayed with him after I lost the first child," she said when she recovered her composure. "I was pregnant again."

She told me how she'd felt a second chance for parenthood as exoneration. Alan had different feelings. "He didn't want the child. He wanted me to abort." But this she adamantly refused to do. He was not overtly hostile at the beginning, limiting his opposition to silence and denial of the pregnancy altogether. She withdrew from him.

"I left our bedroom and lived in a guest room on the other side of the house. He got furious that the child in my womb was beyond his control. I was exhilarated. I had purpose again, something besides daily anger and recrimination; I began to see how sterile my life had become. The child was a gift from Fate, a gift to myself and a gift I could give to the world."

She paused, and we both looked out the window at the harbor. I held her hand across the table.

"We weren't speaking, except he would call me names, 'pig, slut, whore,' those sorts of endearments. He's vindictive. He had come to blame me entirely for the loss of the first child. 'You really believe you're fit to be a parent?' he said to me once. It took my breath away, but this was Alan at his purest, his nastiest.

"One morning I sensed his anger building because I couldn't feel it directly. His tone of voice was calm. He tried to be pleasant, but I had learned he hides hostility when a plan is in process of execution. I wasn't feeling well. The pregnancy had been difficult at the beginning, morning sickness and weariness. Now it was backache. He must have calculated what it would take to rile me. The pain at times was excruciating, but I wouldn't take pills. We were sitting at breakfast and he kept finding pretexts to argue, small, pointless arguments: 'We're out of coffee and butter, I noticed; if you're going to give up on shopping let me know before we run out of toilet paper,' needling me in his mannered unctuous way, so transparently working up to something. 'How long will it take to lose the weight you're gaining?'

" 'All right Alan, that's enough.'

" 'I don't think it is.'

" 'What do you want from me? I don't bother you; I don't talk to you; I don't sleep with you.'

"Maybe that's the point exactly. Maybe that's precisely the point.'

" 'I just want to stay away from you until after the baby is born.'

" 'Let's talk about the baby.'

" 'Let's not.'

" 'You don't say much about it. Why is that?'

" 'I really don't want to get into it.'

" 'Why not? Having a child is a joyful thing.'

" 'I guess I can't get past what happened last time.'

" 'What are you talking about?'

" 'You know exactly what I'm talking about.'

" 'You mean your carelessness? Your negligence? Is that what you're talking about?'

" 'Don't you dare; don't you ever say anything like that to me.'

"And then I picked up the plate and threw it across the room, and the sugar shaker, and the salt- and pepper shakers; I started throwing everything I could get my hands on. He jumped at me and knocked me to the floor. The phony calm manner cracked completely; his face was enraged. He stood over me, kicking me: 'What are you saying, huh? What are you saying, huh?' And each 'huh' was a kick. It went on for at least a minute. I was screaming, trying to get away, but my back spasmed and the pain immobilized me. He kicked and kicked, and I knew while it was happening that this was something he had planned at least unconsciously for a long time, doing again something he knew could end the pregnancy while claiming in his mind I had started it; the guilt he felt from the first miscarriage was pain I had caused him in the end, and that justified any retaliation, even something so extreme as repeating the original crime for a double dose of remorse. He's very sick. I lost the child, of course."

I had trouble comprehending it. "But why would someone, even Alan, go to such grotesque lengths to hurt you and destroy his own child?"

"You don't see it, yet," she said. "It wasn't his child."

"Whose was it?"

"Whose?" Her eyebrows went up. "It was yours."

"*Mine?*"

"And he knew it."

Scales fell from my eyes. *My child?* Shock numbed me, then outrage.

Desire for vengeance settled invincibly on resolve. This was too much. Alan meant to set me up from the beginning. If he was successful I could spend a decade in jail at his instigation.

"We won't call the police, now or ever," I said, weighing the implications of what even then I must have understood as a plan already formulated in the first minute I'd set eyes on Charlotte's beaten face.

I made arrangements for Charlotte to stay at the King's Alley Hotel. I wanted her away from Alan, especially in light of what she'd told me about their life together. I was going to suggest she move in with me, but someone else had other plans.

part four

As I've always said, people with short hair must be told the truth.

—Virginia Woolf

thirty-three

My cell phone rang; it was the call I'd been waiting for.

"Melrose?"

"Your man Alan Lansing is a bad seed."

"Tell me about it."

"The Feds are hot on his tail. You were right: he launders cash big-time. His main connection is a guy named Enrico DaSilva."

"I know DaSilva."

"You know him?"

"He's down here now. I had him and a guy named Bonaventure on a charter."

"DaSilva is a Brazilian who lives near Santo Domingo. Bernard Bonaventure is his lieutenant. Bonaventure arranges transportation for DaSilva: cars, boats, trucks, planes, choppers, whatever. DaSilva's organization moves product from Colombia through Haiti to the Dominican Republic and points north. Lansing is not directly involved in their business, but as you said, he launders their cash. He also bags skim from his partnership, and he's got sturdy investments in the Canadian porn trade. The Feds know he's dirty, but they can't nail him."

"Where is he vulnerable?"

"When his partners find out he's been stealing from them it won't go down well. By the way, did you install the firewall I sent you?"

"Yes. And thanks."

"So you're secure. I'll e-mail you account numbers and balances. There's a lot of activity on those accounts. He shuffles money around, but it will give you an idea. Also, he's into kinky sex. He likes dominant women, girl types, college coeds, that sort of thing. He likes pain and scripted humiliation. If you fight him, don't kick him in the balls; he might fall in love."

"Thanks for the warning."

"Oh, and the DVD. That was courtesy of the Feds."

"The FBI?"

"My guess is they were tailing both him and his wife, caught you in the act, and sent the DVD to him as part of the harassment program. He sent it to you so you'd think he was behind it."

"How close are they to nailing him?"

"It's hard to say. If they have what I have they'll get him soon."

"I won't ask you how you got this."

"It's the information age, man. You can run, but you can never hide."

"How easy is it for you?"

"It's, like, Psychology 101. For instance, you have a number of passwords. One of them is probably N37602."

"You are frightening."

"I mean, like, it's not rocket science. You fly seaplanes. What's the most famous seaplane?

"The Spruce Goose."

"What's the registration number?"

"N37602."

"Hello."

"Good-bye, Melrose."

"Later."

thirty-four

Jason:

For years there was a place on the West Side near the docks where men and women went to indulge in extreme sexual activities publicly. It was largely gay during the week, but on weekends heterosexual couples were welcome to wander the dungeons.

Regulars were known to one another by proclivity: submissives, lesbians, bi-curious housewives from Scarsdale; it was an uncensored, sexually subversive playground of the polymorphous perverse.

Three or four nights a month, Alan Lansing would meet a young woman of twenty-two, an attractive, well-educated, well-spoken, ex-debutante of the type he was familiar with as a young man. They would go to the club. There he would insert a ring through a pierced hole in his penis and change into a leather body harness that trussed his arms tightly to his sides. The woman would then clip a leash to his penis ring and lead him through the club, giving him commands. He often stood at attention for thirty minutes or more before being ordered to move. Sometimes she commanded him to kneel. She rarely had physical contact with him, though she had the power to bring him to orgasm by touching him at certain moments he conveyed by signal. He was rarely erect at the moment of ejaculation. After three hours or more of being led around in this fashion, the pleasure was over. The woman unbound him. He removed the ring, packed up his apparatus, showered, and the two went for a late dinner. He looked radiant after these sessions. I know this to be the truth because the girl is the daughter of a dear friend and I spoke to her personally. She's putting herself through graduate school: a psychology major, what else?

Thought you'd be curious to know.

It's a small world.

Love,
Madeline

I called her right away.

"Are you kidding me?" I said.

She laughed. "The story was first told to me by a gay friend who happened to recognize the girl at a restaurant a few months ago where she and Lansing were having lunch. He'd seen them at the club. I'm close enough to her to get the truth, so I called her and, yes, she's working her way through grad school doing role-play. He pays her five hundred dollars to lead him around on a leash."

"Wow," I said. "Bow-wow!"

It made a perverse kind of sense. Someone who ruthlessly ruined careers enjoyed, in his free time, ruthless humiliations; his ironies collected into bitter farce: a porn king who couldn't have erections, a miser who wouldn't touch money, he couldn't have what he craved, in marriage, in business, in sex, in anything.

"Is this an open secret in New York?"

"I don't think so; I'm not sure. But Jason, I want you to be cautious."

"I'll watch out."

This information and what I got from Melrose Maynard painted an ugly picture. I was well in tune with the psychopathology taking shape in this portrait of Alan Lansing. Individuals drawn to power are prone to perversions their dignity cannot abide; one side of their character simply denies the proclivities of the other until they find themselves in situations that are criminal, ridiculous, or both. Each episode of violent abuse widened the divide between how he wanted to seem and who he really was, increasing both his self-hatred and his aggression. Alan Lansing projected his dysfunctions onto a world that finally mirrored all his fear and loathing. This made him a dangerous man.

thirty-five

I walked down the narrow road at the end of my drive to the familiar path at the bottom of the hill. The path ran through high Bahamas grass where it ended abruptly at a broken wooden gate through which lay the white sands and calm waters of a well-concealed cove beach. There I spent quiet time reading and thinking in the sun. When the cool part of morning was over, I packed up my collapsible chair, slung it over my shoulder, put my books and towels in the leather half-day bag, and walked the path back to my apartment to shower before lunch. I planned to meet Charlotte in the afternoon.

I climbed the stairs at home two at a time. When I got to the top I went through the door and took a quick step to the left to toss my bag in the corner. Standing there with a grin on his face was the hatchet-faced mugger I'd smashed on the head with the driftwood club. He was still showing a bruise. In the corner opposite was a dark-skinned mulatto. Short, stocky, built like a fireplug, his neck covered with sunburst tattoos, pronounced frontal lobes gave him a permanent frown and a simian aspect. None of this was good.

"What are you doing here?" I said.

The hatchet face rubbed his bruise. The one I didn't know pulled a gun. "Mr. DaSilva," he said, "requests the pleasure of your company."

Without warning, the hatchet face wheeled around and smashed my gut with a spring-loaded blackjack. I went down in tremendous pain, gasping. It took all the fight out of me. Both of the men helped me down the stairs to their car. It was parked behind the building. The fireplug sat beside me in the backseat, his gun in my ribs. I felt sick.

I was taken to an area south of Fredriksted that extends out to a wooded peninsula surrounded by isolated beaches. The dirt road off the main route was cratered and bumpy; the driver was going just fast enough to make the ride as uncomfortable as it could be. We stopped in front of a small wooden house. Paint was peeling from the clapboard sideboards and the screen was torn on the front porch.

"Get out."

The driver walked me to the house, up two wooden steps to the porch. The screen door slammed behind us. The other man knocked on the front door. It opened and we went in.

"Hello, Bernard," I said. He was standing in the middle of the room.

Bernard's smile was showing big teeth. "Captain," he said, "my apologies. The circumstances are urgent. I don't like coercion. Nobody does."

"What do you want, Bernard? Why am I here?"

"I provide transportation for the organization I work for. I need your cooperation. I've got a package, several packages, that need to be delivered to a ship at a certain location."

"Drugs?"

Bernard waved off the comment. "It doesn't matter what the packages contain. We're only concerned with efficient delivery and discretion. Your plane is a fine machine for the sort of deliveries that are important to Mr. DaSilva's business."

"I'm not interested."

He shrugged. "I'm sorry to insist, Captain Walker. I personally find violence distasteful; the need to resort to threats is a failure of professionalism." He raised his eyebrows and looked down. "Sometimes, however, expedience overrules diplomacy. This is one of those instances. I beg your indulgence."

His gentleman's manner was unconvincing.

"Is this your place?" I asked him, looking at the shabby walls. The house had all the charm of lonely old age; it was large but drab and furnished with old rattan chairs and faded blue pillows. The couch had a broken leg on one end that sat on a stack of *National Geographic* magazines. The shades were pulled down and dirty lace curtains gave the room a depressing aura of blasted hope.

Bernard read my thoughts and laughed. "Quite right. You see, we all have to make sacrifices."

"What do you want me to do?" I might as well ask; I could see no way out.

"Here's what we need. . . ."

Bernard Bonaventure spoke for five minutes. He opened a nautical chart and outlined a rendezvous point fifty miles south of St. Croix. I would land the *Clipper* there beside a motor yacht waiting for the drop; a launch would come to us and we'd hand over the cargo.

"Tonight at nine o'clock," he said.

"You're talking about landing in the open ocean after dark?"

"The plane was designed for that. You told me so yourself."

"You've got too much confidence in me, Bernard. There's a lot of risk; you've got wind and waves to worry about, and swells; darkness doubles the difficulty."

"I have my orders." Bernard was adamant. "Make it work. These gentlemen will accompany us and see that you do."

The door in the corner opened and a woman I recognized from the charter as the one in the yellow bikini came into the room. She wore a white cotton blouse and a white wraparound dress.

"Hello, Captain," she said. "I am Maria; do you remember me?"

I nodded.

"Join us for cocktails, my dear," Bernard said.

"I am sorry for this," she said, with obvious distaste; kidnapping was outside her definition of good grace. Her eyes were honest and sad; she had the look of a woman waiting for a simple life of normal expectations she knew would never be hers.

"Here you are, my dear," Bernard said, handing her a tall red drink. His manner was oversolicitous and she smiled with a strained expression; they were giving a performance of politeness, like a couple entertaining neighbors after a domestic squabble.

Bernard started talking about his early days in Ecuador. The scene reminded me of the movie *Key Largo* when Johnny Rocco is having a shave, telling everyone how big he was in Chicago as the barber sculpts his shaving cream into the face of a clown.

I knew this was the set-up Charlotte had warned me about. I also knew I had to get away. The afternoon passed slowly. I kept an eye on the weather. The wind was stronger than usual. By seven o'clock the sun had already set.

A panel truck pulled up to the house and Bernard told his men to get ready. He escorted me out. The truck was filled with packages wrapped in burlap. I didn't want to know what was inside them. We drove to the ramp. The truck stopped by the rear door to unload.

"I've got to preflight," I told them. Bernard nodded. The skies were overcast; it would be dark soon. I unlocked the plane and climbed up on the wing to check the fuel and oil.

I was standing between the engines when I saw the bow hatch open. Johnny's head bobbed up. He had a big smile on his face when he saw me; Yarrow bobbed up behind him and I knew what they were up to. I put a finger to my lips and motioned them down. Bernard and the others were in back loading the plane and couldn't see ahead. I slid down the windscreen to the bow hatch.

"Johnny, listen up. I've been hijacked by Enrico DaSilva and Bernard." His eyes got big as banjos. "Get the handheld radio and standby on frequency 123.45. They want me to meet a ship fifty miles south of here to make a drop. I'm going to try to get loose somehow. Wait to hear from me. I'll go back and distract them; you two jump and run."

Johnny took it all in. I didn't have a plan, but at least someone knew my plight.

I went back along the top of the fuselage, climbed down the utility steps at the rear entry, and swung into the cabin; Bernard and the driver were stacking the packages.

"You can't just throw this cargo anywhere," I told them, with an edge in my voice. "It has to be put forward for weight and balance. Here, put it over there."

When they were finished I went forward and crawled through the cockpit catwalk to the bow compartment to be sure Johnny and Yarrow were gone. The compartment was empty. I closed the hatch.

"Get rid of the truck and get back here, pronto," Bernard told the driver. "Hector will also be coming with us," he said.

"You're the babysitter?" I said to the hatchet-faced man. So his name was Hector. He grinned but said nothing. I knew from Hector's dead eyes that I was dead if I couldn't get away from them before the job was finished. They did big business with

Alan Lansing and probably owed him a favor; I was useful and then expendable; he was killing two birds with one stone, a phrase I wished hadn't occurred to me.

When the other one was aboard, I pulled the ladder up and checked that the doors were locked and the cargo was secure enough not to shift in flight. I told the driver where to sit, then went into the cockpit and strapped in. "You ride in the co-pilot's seat," I told Bernard. I said to Hector, "You sit behind him." Hector was basic; he didn't look much like he enjoyed the idea of flying in any seat. I ran through the checklist slowly and methodically, mouthing each item, trying to emphasize the complexity of the airplane. I knew the cockpit looked like a maze of clocks to the untrained eye. A plan was germinating, but I didn't quite have it yet.

thirty-six

After I started the engines, I programmed the GPS for the rendezvous coordinates Bernard had given me. Dusk was quickly turning to dark. The wind was blowing steady and strong. The harbor was protected by a reef, so the waves were slight, even in moderate winds. The ocean would be a different story. I taxied down the ramp and into the water and turned the landing light on to scan the takeoff track. After the safety checks we were ready to go. I turned into the wind and eased the throttles up to full power. Once on the step, the *Clipper* accelerated smoothly to a normal takeoff.

The GPS indicated a 172-degree bearing for twenty-one minutes. I climbed to five hundred feet. We headed south along the western side of the island. The moon had not risen and beaches on the Sandy Point peninsula were hard to make out.

Once clear to the south of the island I descended to two

hundred feet, turned on the landing light, and began to study the water. Swells were broad and evenly spaced but perpendicular to the wind line; touchdown would be a complicated maneuver. It looked to me like a crosswind approach parallel to the swells was the best strategy. The sea is ever changing and unforgiving; it's a force with imperatives indifferent to difficulty.

The technique for rough-water landings involves slowing the airboat down to within a few knots of stalling speed with high power and full flaps. This allows you to "hang it on the prop" and fly just above the waves looking for a place that appears to be flat. You then reduce power to stall the plane into the water, put the throttles into reverse thrust, retract the flaps, and the airboat will stop in as little as three hundred feet. The greater problem comes at takeoff. It's difficult to accelerate on uneven waters; the waves are violent as you gain speed. A crosswind makes it worse. Sometimes it takes more than one attempt to get airborne safely.

We approached the rendezvous point. I saw the lights of a motor yacht at twelve o'clock.

"That's the ship," Bernard said.

I flashed the landing light and made a wide left turn to orbit the ship and analyze the seas. Once into the wind I extended fifteen degrees of flaps, slowing to 105 knots. The water was rough and it was going to be ugly, but I didn't say anything to Bernard. He'd find out soon enough.

I put out thirty and then forty degrees of flaps, adding power as we got close to the waves. The ship signaled us with a flashing light.

I saw fear on Bernard's face as the roughness of the seas became apparent. I waited until the ship was just off our port beam and dropped the Albatross in. We hit hard, but I put the flaps up, went into reverse, and we slowed quickly.

We bobbed up and down as I turned the *Clipper* against the swells. I taxied slowly crosswind toward the ship, using the upwind throttle to compensate for the tendency of the airboat to weathercock.

Bernard got on his cell phone. After a brief exchange he snapped it shut. He turned to me. "They're sending a launch."

"It's going to be tricky." I looked at Hector. His hatchet face was green with misery. Seasickness happens quickly. The pitch and roll of the Albatross was pronounced; waves were breaking over the bow. "Use the sick sack," I said. He did.

I stayed downwind of the yacht with the engines running. The launch was a large inflatable, which was the only practical vessel for ship-to-ship transfer in these waters. As it approached I shut down the engines and went back to open the rear hatch. There were two men in the launch. I signaled them to approach and told them to throw me a line. I made the line fast to the port side of the fuselage. Bernard, Hector, and the other one began to untie the cargo stays. Bernard seemed immune to the sickening motion.

Each package was wrapped in burlap and about the size of two basketballs, and there were about thirty packages stacked like cordwood. It took them fifteen minutes to transfer all the bundles. When they were done, Bernard said, "I'll be leaving you now. Wait here. The launch will return with cargo for another drop."

"Another drop?"

"Another ship is waiting for cargo we will presently load."

"Where?"

He smiled again. "You'll be given new coordinates. Hector and Sanchez will wait with you. Thank you for your cooperation."

I held the bow fast while Bernard jumped aboard. Then the launch backed off and they were gone.

Hector looked miserable and Sanchez not much better. The work of transferring cargo had put their minds off sickness, but now Hector was ill again.

"Let me see if I've got some medicine," I told him. He waved at me miserably. I went back to the cockpit and turned on the radio. The airline common frequency in Caribbean airspace is 123.45. Johnny would be standing by on the handheld. I couldn't speak to him directly, but I could have an airliner relay. I picked up the microphone:

"Any airline, this is Albatross 7026 Charlie."

"Go ahead, Albatross; this is American 951."

"American 951, can you relay a message to Island Air Operations on this frequency?"

"Roger, Albatross, go ahead with your message."

"First delivery made. Proceeding to unscheduled second station. Request you stand by this frequency for waypoint info."

"Copy that. Stand by for relay."

I listened while American 951 relayed my request.

"Albatross 26 Charlie, American 951."

"Albatross 26 Charlie, go ahead."

"Roger, 26 Charlie, Island Ops advises standing by and Mitch says hello."

"Thanks for your help, American."

"Roger."

Johnny had Mitch ready to go into action. I needed a way to get free. There was a solution, I was sure of it; I was puzzling that when the launch returned.

thirty-seven

I squinted into the light shining from the bow of the returning launch as I caught the line. Enrico DaSilva stepped off into the *Clipper's* cabin.

"Good evening, Captain," he said.

DaSilva was all business. His intense eyes darted this way and that. He was highly strung when he wasn't relaxing.

He gave orders to Hector and the other one in Spanish. They transferred two travel trunks from the launch. The seas were rough; I told them to make the trunks secure in the forward cabin. I didn't want them getting loose. Enrico and I went to the cockpit to talk.

"Here are the coordinates for the next rendezvous," he said, handing me a slip of paper. "We are going to fly to another ship where you will leave me and the cargo."

The point was about seventy-five miles north of our present position.

My mind was working fast and efficiently. The military teaches you to define objectives, prioritize response, and formulate solutions based on available resources. Objective: to thwart the enemy's intent. Objective: to recapture command of the ship. Objective: to secure my own freedom and safety.

"It will take about forty-five minutes to get there," Enrico said.

"What are you going to do with me? Let me go?" I had to ask, just to see how he'd respond.

"You will be well taken care of, and we will, of course, rely on your discretion."

"What assurance do I have?"

"You have my word," he said quietly. His expression relaxed for a moment to enjoy the deceit. I was a dead man. My mind ran on—objective: reverse the control.

When we were ready I closed the hatch and went back to the cockpit. I put Enrico in the co-pilot's seat and told the two others to sit in the cabin.

"I need them there for weight and balance," I explained.

Enrico nodded.

I closed the cockpit door and strapped in and began to run the checklist. Whitecaps broke over the bow.

thirty-eight

The Albatross pitched and rolled on the waves. I went through the checklist slowly to give seasickness a chance to grab Enrico. It didn't take long.

"Are we going to start the engines soon?" he said impatiently.

"Just about to do that now."

I turned on the switches and pressed the starters in sequence; both engines fired up. Engines running, I taxied off the wind; waves continued to break over the bow from the port beam. I had anger's courage. This was going to be one terrifying take-off; I'd see to that.

The landing light gave me two hundred feet of visibility, but spray over the bow obstructed vision. It would get worse in the first stage of takeoff. I elected to run a quartering left crosswind on a track parallel to the main swells.

"Ready?" I said to Enrico. He looked uncertain. "Here we go."

I advanced the left throttle first to keep us tracking against the tendency of the airplane to weathercock in the crosswind. The waves slammed against the hull as we picked up speed. A swell passed across the bow and we rose dramatically up and down again. I held the control wheel firmly back to keep the bow up. As the flight controls became effective against the wind, I brought the right throttle forward and we had full power. As our speed increased, waves and spray appeared rapidly and suddenly in the dark. We rode up on another swell and I drove the bow down slightly in the trough. We reached forty knots, but a large wave sent us into the air prematurely; the plane heaved up; I held the control wheel back, waiting for impact. It came, violently. We hit another wave and were thrown up again, and this time we began to porpoise. As I held steady back pressure on the wheel and hard right rudder, the porpoise stabilized. Approaching sixty-five knots, the airboat rose on another swell; I pulled briskly back on the control wheel and at last we were airborne.

Smooth air in flight made a striking contrast to the harrowing takeoff. I was smiling to myself. Enrico was unprepared for that kind of excitement; it had shaken him up, and that's exactly what I wanted. Enrico's men came running up to the cockpit yammering in Spanish. They were scared to death. Fine, I thought.

"Tell them to get back in their seats and stay there until you tell them to get up," I told Enrico. He nodded, spoke to them sternly in Spanish. They nodded solemnly and went back to their seats. I closed the cockpit door after them.

The GPS bearing to the rendezvous waypoint was 354 degrees. I picked up that heading. In forty-three minutes we'd be there. I was planning a landing that would be as memorable as the takeoff.

thirty-nine

The wind was out of the east at a velocity I estimated to be twenty-five knots. The GPS had us five miles from the rendezvous when I saw the lights of another ship at twelve o'clock.

"Is that it?" I said to DaSilva.

He nodded.

I dropped down to five hundred feet. "This is going to be rough," I said. He didn't want to hear that. I orbited the motor yacht, a large private pleasure cruiser. They signaled with a light, as the first ship had; I signaled by flashing my landing light and positioned myself for final approach to the east, into the wind. The swells were not as pronounced in this area, but the waves were high enough. I was well practiced in rough-water technique. Objective: make use of all available resources. By now I had my plan: I meant to let the sea and the airboat terrorize Enrico and his thugs.

I turned into the wind and put out thirty, then forty degrees of flaps. As we neared the surface, whitecaps were apparent. We flew just above them. I watched Enrico's reaction. He was smart enough to be scared. I brought the hull to within two feet of the crests, pushed the power up, and we flew across what looked like a small mountain range of water. Trimming off control wheel pressures, I checked power, then eased the yoke slightly forward to drop the bow. The hull slammed into a wave, giving us a tremendous shock. Ordinarily I'd land at this point. Instead I added full throttle to maintain flying speed; the bow rose up; I eased the power off and went down again and slammed into the next crest. Enrico had not attached his crotch strap. The violent impact sent him under his seat belt, nearly out of his seat entirely; he was trapped, with the belt under his arms and around his chest. I slammed the plane again, marveling at the Grumman's ability to take this kind of punishment. Enrico squirmed in panic, tangled in his belt. After the fourth and most violent impact yet, a bone-jarring smash that sent spray over the windscreen, it was enough. I pushed the throttles to full power and climbed to five hundred feet.

Enrico, terrified and disorientated, was trying to struggle back into his seat. I reached for the fire extinguisher on the floor beside me, unclipped it, pulled the pin, and fired a blast of halon gas into his face. His last breath of oxygen vented as a scream lost in the howl of the engines. I slammed his forehead with the blunt end of the fire bottle and he went unconscious. I grabbed his gun and headed for Christiansted Harbor.

forty

I had to put myself in a killing frame of mind. I felt sure the men in back were frightened enough not to leave their seats until after we landed. Lethal force was the safest course of action. Reluctantly, I resolved to use it.

With the lights of Christiansted ahead I set flaps and began a descent for landing. I came in low over the reef and made a smooth touchdown, in great contrast to the drama of the open ocean. I steered for the middle of the channel and put the landing gear down to keep the Clipper as slow as possible, then put the left propeller into idle reverse. Now the ship went into a tight left circular pattern. This allowed me to get out of the seat without raising suspicion in the back.

Enrico was alive but still unconscious. I turned him over and took his belt, looped it twice around each bicep with no slack, and secured it in a manner taught to me by my aunt Madeline one antic afternoon.

Once that was done I examined his pistol, a Desert Eagle XIX .44 Magnum assault weapon, as deadly a handgun as existed. I made sure the safety was off and the clip was loaded. I remembered from Air Force days that the kick on a weapon like this was substantial. I'd have to be careful to keep the barrel lower than seemed right; otherwise I'd be shooting up the ceiling and they'd have time to drop me, which is what nearly happened.

Once I was sure the gun was ready to fire, I had to psych myself for the assault. I stood at the cockpit door, rage building in me. I thought about Charlotte and what had happened to her, and about the mugging, and about a series of small intimidations in the past year I could now attribute to Alan. Finally, I thought about the truth of what had happened here, that I had been hijacked and marked to be murdered, and how after this was finished I'd pay a visit to Alan Lansing. He had taken me out of my skin, and before I returned to a civilized frame of mind I would greet him as the creature he'd conjured.

I was ready. I counted down from ten, and as I did I willfully shook off my sanity. At the end of the countdown I threw open the cockpit door and stepped into the cabin with the gun.

The driver, Sanchez, looked up expecting to see Enrico. His eyes flashed toward the running engines, recognizing in an instant that it was a diversion. When he saw the muzzle of my gun leveled at his gut, he realized that Enrico was dead or disabled; his left eyebrow twitched slightly in final epiphany as I fired; he fell backward.

The other one, Hector, in a torpor of seasickness, had come to his senses, stood up, and was reaching for his weapon. I pointed at him and fired. The gun recoiled violently and I missed. There was shock and fury in his eyes. He raised his pistol and I sidestepped;

he fired and missed. I dropped to my knees, sighted him low, and pulled the trigger, aiming at his gut. The round hit the left side of his head in a violent spray of pink blood and bone. He was dead before he hit the floor.

forty-one

Killing is like sex you feel ashamed about afterward. I went back to the cockpit dazed and numb. I got back into the seat and steered for the ramp, brought the Albatross up, and parked it. Once the engines were shut down, a deep silence descended.

I sat silently for a moment. What had happened and why? I had two corpses and a prisoner on board, and two trunks of something everyone had risked a lot to get. I went back to the cabin to find out what I was carrying.

A sickly odor of illness and death greeted me when I went through the cabin door. The first one I'd killed was lying near the trunks. His mouth was open. His face had that marble pallor of a fresh corpse and his eyes looked sightlessly upward. I stepped over him, knelt in front of the first trunk, and snapped the latch with a screwdriver. When I opened it a shudder went down my spine. It was filled with dense packets of hundred-dollar bills, at least 1, maybe 2 million dollars. It wasn't what I expected and was not what I wanted to see. Money like that brings nothing but bad luck.

I closed the trunk and stood to survey the damage. The cabin looked like a charnel house. The one with half his head gone had bled all over. Both of them had been sick. I saw where the second bullet had gone through the top of the hull.

All of it was trouble I had to deal with tonight, but first I had unfinished business with Alan Lansing.

forty-two

My weapon was a 12-gauge Remington under-and-over, double barrels sawed off at the breech, its stock cut down to a pistol grip, simple, unambiguous, deadly. I shoved it down my belt and left my apartment. When I turned into the driveway I felt calm. I got out of the car, both my hands visible.

Alan chose precisely this moment to come out of the house by the side door. He was carrying a transparent bag of recyclables, a number of scotch bottles, I happened to notice. I was the last person he expected to see. Startled, his head turned sideways and up, the way a dog's does when it would ask a question if it could speak.

We stood about twenty feet apart. He put the bag down. The bottles in it made a clanking jangle; he backed up slightly. We appraised each other and there was that tense silence with everything in it as he realized his assumptions about me were wrong.

"Look," he said finally. "This is ridiculous. What are you doing here?"

"You set me up."

I pulled the gun out and leveled it at his gut. He stared at it in frightened wonder like an altar boy at a leering priest.

"Do you believe in God, Alan?" My eyes raged with madness. I jerked the gun rapidly toward the door.

"Don't do this—"

"Let's go inside."

When he got to the door he paused and looked back at me.

"Open it," I said. He opened it slowly and I followed him into the kitchen. "Turn off the lights."

"We can work this out," he said.

"How? If I let you live, Charlotte and I die. And I don't want to kill you; that would be wrong. We'll have to think of something else. It's war, Alan; you declared it. A warrior must be prepared to die. You know that."

"You're insane."

"We're more alike than you think. Upstairs."

"—?"

"Your study."

"Why not talk here?"

"Upstairs." I shoved the gun at his gut.

Alan couldn't fathom me; he was bewildered. He turned; I kept the gun at his back. We went through the kitchen and down the hall to the stairs. The study was at the end of the hall on the second floor. It was dimly lit. He kept hesitating, oddly reluctant to go in. I found out why soon enough.

An exercise machine was positioned behind his desk. A noose was hanging from a pull bar over his chair. The desk was covered with pornography, some of it clearly underage stuff. Amyl nitrate poppers littered the floor.

"Having a party?"

His eyes glowered. I picked up a photograph, looked at the

noose, and shook my head, then moved around him to the desk chair; I pushed the makeshift gallows away and shoved the pictures to the floor, then sat in his chair with the shotgun pointed squarely at his chest.

"Close the blinds," I said. "Keep your hands visible to me and make all your movements slow." He did as I asked. I pointed to a chair near the gun collection. "Pull that over here and sit down."

His eyes stayed fixed on mine, struggling to gauge my intent, resolve.

Murder has no access to higher sensibilities; vengeance is pure adrenaline. Watch a man's hands to take his measure, not his eyes. I felt calm.

"Take your gun out of the case and break it open. Shake out the shells and shove it across the desk."

He did what I told him to do; the rounds clattered across the desktop and he slid the pistol over to me.

"Here are the rules. One in the cylinder, the cylinder is spun. You put the gun in your mouth and pull the trigger. If it goes click, then it's my turn."

"You're out of your mind."

"Maybe."

I pulled both triggers back to full-cock. He flinched. I leaned across the desk and looked him straight in the eye.

"This is important. If you try to take a shot at me I'll kill you. Do you understand?" I sat back in the chair. "Oh, wait; one other matter: you've got to write a note. Use this. I'll tell you what to say." I pushed a page of his stationery and a pen across the desk.

"No. I won't do it."

He was staring into the double muzzles.

"This is how I want it to read. . . ."

Offshore trusts in the Cayman Islands were to go to Charlotte, and a trust in Nevis was to be established for the families of pensioners of four companies he'd helped to destroy. Melrose

Maynard had hacked Alan's accounts and I had all the numbers in my head. My knowledge of his financial affairs shocked him.

Alan wrote it all out, signed it, then threw the pen and the note on the desk.

He had pretty penmanship. I was frankly surprised he was so compliant, but the persuasive power of a shotgun can never be underrated.

He watched while I broke the cylinder completely out of the .38 and inserted a round. Then I placed a prefitted circle of thin black opaque paper over the cylinder's business end.

"This way, Alan, neither of us can peek and cheat."

I waved the loaded cylinder in his face; I put the gun down.

I pushed the .38 to the center of the desk. "You can spin it yourself if you want to."

"Fuck you."

"Whatever you say. Nonetheless, one of us has to die."

"You're bluffing. You've got everything to lose and nothing to gain."

I sighed theatrically, picked up the gun, put it to my head, and pulled the trigger.

Click.

I broke the cylinder, spun it, reinserted it, and pushed the gun across the desk. "Now it's your turn."

He looked at me with a deeply puzzled expression, then looked at the gun; his face was red and contorted. I had never seen anything like it except in lovemaking. My eyes burned into his. He picked up the gun, put it into his mouth, closed his eyes, and pulled the trigger.

Click.

He opened his eyes. An utterly startled expression came over him. He was sweating and breathing heavily.

"Now it's my turn. Put the gun on the desk." I broke the cylinder, spun it again, and snapped it back.

Alan had hope. He had called my bluff. He watched my eyes

for the tell, but all he saw was resolve. He didn't understand larger purpose or risk; he didn't understand good and evil; but mainly, he didn't understand himself, and that made him incapable of understanding anyone. I picked up the revolver, put it to my head, and pulled the trigger.

Click.

Alan began to weep. He looked like a condemned man.

"The game's not over, Alan," I said. I broke the cylinder again, spun it, and tossed him the gun.

"No," he said.

"We have to keep playing."

He took the gun up suddenly, pointed it at me, and pulled the trigger.

Click.

I was on my feet with the shotgun at his head. He froze, dropped the gun.

"Must you cheat at everything? Pick the gun up, Alan. Pick it up and put it into your mouth. You don't get to spin it this time."

I thought he was going to be sick, but he did what I asked him to do. Trembling, he put the gun into his mouth. His eyes stared into mine. He knew this was the shot. The moment was charged with the pure certain truth of death. But then . . .

. . . Alan fell back into the chair. He put the gun down and began to cry.

"Don't kill me; don't make me do this, please, please." I looked at him with astonishment. His face assumed an aspect of mawkish pleading. I had never seen a man become so abject so suddenly and unexpectedly. It filled me with disgust.

I leaned over and whispered, "I know who you are, and what you are. Now pull the trigger, Alan. This one's for all the people you've fucked over in your brief, unfruitful time on earth, and for two unborn children who didn't get a chance."

"No."

"Take the shot."

He looked up at me. His eyes had a sudden brilliance in them, as if a truthful part of his mind had awakened to miraculous understanding. He raised the gun slowly, and as it got closer to his mouth, a quizzical expression passed across his features. Then he closed his eyes as the barrel went in. The gunshot sounded with a spray of blood exploding against the wall. His body lurched backward and slumped into the chair; then he tumbled forward facedown on the floor over the photographs I'd pushed from the desk, the gun near his ankle. There was deathly silence after that, and into the still air of the room settled the odor of gunpowder and excrement and blood.

forty-three

Adrenaline was pumping. I had to get back to the plane. I needed help with the problems I'd left behind on the ramp. I dialed up Johnny; his cell phone put me into voice mail. "It's Jason. Call me." Sixty seconds later my phone rang.

"Where are you?" Johnny said.

"On my way back to the ramp. Meet me there."

"Are you okay?"

"I'm fine."

"I'll see you in five minutes."

"Don't board until I'm with you."

"I've got Mitch Holden with me."

"Bring him."

I closed the phone and headed down toward the boardwalk. Lights along the harbor were a deceptively peaceful sight, greatly at odds with my mood. The Albatross cabin was a mess of murder; Enrico DaSilva was still alive, and there was serious money to be dealt with.

When I got to the ramp it was past midnight. Johnny and Mitch were standing by the bow. They saw me coming.

"What the hell happened?" Johnny said.

"I was hijacked earlier this afternoon by DaSilva and the same people who mugged me in June. Two of them are dead inside and DaSilva's tied up. There are two trunks in the cabin with, I figure, one or two million dollars in hundred-dollar bills."

"Ho-ly shit," Johnny said, wide eyes white with wonder.

"Who is DaSilva?" Mitch's head was cocked; he was calm and curious as a cat.

"He runs drugs. Alan Lansing launders money for him and his organization. They had me fly a load to a ship south of here. We made the delivery and got the money. At the next drop I was able to put DaSilva out and get his gun."

"How did you do that?" Johnny said.

"I scared him on the rough waters, grabbed the fire bottle, and shot him with halon."

"That'll do it," Mitch said, with a grin of admiration.

"I smashed him with the empty bottle for good measure and tied him up; he's on the floor in the cockpit. The other two were seasick in the cabin. After I landed in the channel I came out firing and got them both. It's a fucking mess in there. I wanted to prepare you for what you're going to see."

"I saw you in the channel turning circles and heard the shots," said Mitch.

"Let's go inside," I said.

I went up the ladder into the cabin. Mitch and Johnny were right behind me. The hatchet-faced gunman missing half his head was slumped in the corner. Johnny, wide-eyed, tried to absorb the scene. He walked forward and hovered over the body by the trunks of money.

Mitch was about to say something when suddenly the cockpit

door flew open. Enrico was free. He was holding the flare gun. I fell to the floor as it flashed; the light was blinding; the flare sizzled past my head and exploded against the aft bulkhead above me. Mitch reached for his knife. I rolled to the fire extinguisher by the rear hatch, unhooked it, and emptied it against the burning fabric. Johnny stepped aside as Mitch sprang forward. Enrico was trying to reload, but Mitch flew through the air in a deadly pirouette, plunging the knife into his gut in one continuous motion. Enrico fell against him. His eyes moved to me, and to Johnny, and to the trunks of cash, and finally to Mitch; wonder, disbelief, comprehension, and resignation played across his features; after that he went funny the way boxers get when they don't know what's happening anymore or who they are: his eyes went up, his legs got slack, and Mitch let him drop.

I picked up the flare pistol and put it back in the cockpit. The plane smelled of fire, but the damage was superficial.

"Well, mate, now what?" Mitch wiped his knife on Enrico's jacket.

"I haven't the faintest idea." It was true. "Have a look at the cash."

Mitch stood by while Johnny opened the trunk.

"Wow," Johnny said. Mitch whistled. Money has an effect on people; they either love it or fear it. I guess I fear it. I looked at that money like it had a disease.

"That's a lot more than two million dollars, mate."

"I don't want any part of it," I said.

"That's five million at least. And you've got another trunk with the same amount."

"Ten million dollars!"

"At least. You can't hand it over to the police." Mitch threw out his hands. "It would disappear, and there would be awkward questions to answer. Remember, mate, I've got blood on my hands now, too."

"What are we going to do?" Johnny asked.

Mitch gave me that scrutinizing look of an alpha animal taking measure, a look that summarized what we knew about each other. When he spoke, his tone was serious.

"I grew up sailing in Brisbane. I met a lot of people of all stripes. In a former life I did a bit of contract work," he said, "smuggling, you could say, mainly in the Pacific. I have connections in Indonesia that could absorb this kind of cash."

I looked hard at him. "What are you saying, Mitch, that we should keep it?"

"If you want me to take it on, I'll stash the whole load on my boat. I'll take the bodies, too, get rid of them tomorrow. I'm leaving here at sunup."

"Where are you headed?"

"The Far East, eventually. But not right away. I'm going to take my time. We're not in a rush. The authorities may not be aware of the money, and DaSilva's people aren't going to tell them about it. But there is one important question."

"What is it?"

"Why should you trust me?"

I laughed. There was more money here than we could imagine, and more trouble if word of it got out. Mitch was offering a solution. I gave him an appraising stare. Mitch was strong, independent, subversive, and cool, with a rare quality of leadership based on ferocious self-interest. Eye met eye in silence. Eye met eye in agreement.

"I trust you because you saved my life. And you've got blood on your hands." I looked at Johnny. "We all do. Besides, if I never see the money again, that's fine with me; I just want it gone. But we have to agree here tonight that what happened here never happened. A solemn understanding."

"You're going to sail from here across the Pacific?" Johnny said.

232 · · · tom casey · · · · · · · ·

"*Threshold's* fully capable, Old Son. Your share will be safe."

"My share?" Events kept whirling around Johnny; I smiled at his mystification.

"A three-way split. What do you think, Jason?"

"Fine."

"It will take a few months. I'll contact you from time to time and give you progress reports. We'll plan to meet in Hong Kong in, say, six months. By then I should have things organized."

Johnny looked stunned.

"Agreed?" Mitch looked at Johnny. We put our hands together on it. Each person spoke the word, and a covenant was made.

Then we got busy.

We loaded the money into the Zodiac and shuttled from the ramp to *Threshold*. It took about half an hour to get it all into Mitch's hold. Then we took the bodies, one at a time. I had garbage bags in the hangar. We wrapped them with speed tape. They were heavy and awkward to carry, and we almost lost one over the side.

By four in the morning we were done.

"Well, mate," Mitch said, as we shook hands perhaps for the last time, "I'll be off in an hour. See you in Hong Kong." Something in his smile made me almost believe everything would work out.

Johnny and I went back to the *Clipper* and spent the rest of the night cleaning the cabin, scrubbing the sole with antiseptic. Every so often Johnny would pause and shake his head. "What just happened to us?" he said.

"Nothing," I told him.

forty-four

The authorities were not entirely sure that Alan's death had been a suicide, but they had no evidence to indicate otherwise; there were no traces of my presence in the house that couldn't be explained benignly. As someone who had been to the house on the night of his death, I volunteered to come down to the police station. Inside, I told the desk sergeant why I was there; he buzzed me through a door with thick bulletproof glass and an electric lock. Then the sergeant led me past the holding cells down a hallway to a small interrogation room. I sat alone for a few minutes, until Inspector Paul Lévesque came in and introduced himself. I can still see his burly face and genial smile, a smile that belied strong suspicion in his eyes.

There are three federal marshals on St. Croix; they augment the police force, but in fact they are the larger law. Fugitives think the islands are a haven; federal officers are aware of this and wait patiently for them to show up.

"Just for the record, you are Jason Walker."

"I am."

"And you live where?"

I told him.

He said the police had questioned everyone who had been to the house that day. "You were the last person to see Mr. Lansing alive."

"I guess I was."

"Was there anyone else at the house?"

"He appeared to be alone."

"Were you inside the house?"

"Yes, briefly."

The Inspector sat back, leaning to the side, watching me with that professional aspect of suspicious appraisal that seeks to avoid seeming malevolent.

"Did you go upstairs?"

"No. We stood in the kitchen for a minute or two."

"How did Mr. Lansing seem?"

"He had been drinking, but he seemed normal."

"Normal how? Cheerful? Depressed?"

"He had just taken the garbage out. Bottles, actually. We met in the driveway and he invited me in for a moment."

Inspector Lévesque was not at all sure about me. I could feel it. His eyes seemed friendly, that official menacing sort of friendliness. He reminded me of a hungry bear with a memory of meat. "Why were you there? Were you a friend of Mr. Lansing's?"

"We had a cordial relationship. His wife and I are friendly. I was there to get a book she wanted. She had asked me to pick it up for her if I could. She didn't want to see him." This was a true statement that Charlotte could verify. She was being facetious at the time, but that was as good an excuse as any I could think of. Alan wasn't around to challenge it.

"They were not on good terms?"

"No. She had left him. They were planning to divorce. He was bitter about it."

"Why did she leave him?"

"You'd have to ask Mrs. Lansing."

"How long were you in the house with Mr. Lansing?"

"About five minutes. As I said, he seemed normal. I heard the shot as I stood in the driveway."

"Why were you standing in the driveway?"

"I was walking away. I stopped when I heard the shot."

"Why didn't you call the police?"

"I didn't know it was a shot at the time. It was a noise, that's all. He was alone. I didn't think it was anything."

That was all I would tell him. It was enough. He folded his hands and rested them on the desk.

"What do you know about Bill and Emily Schaffer?"

The question flew like a curveball.

"Not much. Steady clients. Good people."

"Emily Schaffer has vanished. On the night of Alan Lansing's death. Her husband is quite upset. There was a lot he didn't know about his wife."

"Such as?"

"Such as she's been a fugitive from justice for nearly ten years."

"What for?"

"Kidnapping and armed robbery." The Inspector resumed his slouch. "Ten years ago she and a boyfriend kidnapped a man, the estranged husband of a friend of hers. He had been abusing their child; when the abuse became known he fled. With the child. Emily and her boyfriend tracked him down, rescued the girl. But they kidnapped him, robbed him of thirty thousand dollars, and left him tied up in a motel room."

"Alive?"

"He was alive. With an ax handle—well, inconveniently on his person."

"What happened to the child?"

"The mother got her back."

"The money?"

"We don't know. Emily and her boyfriend disappeared."

"Maybe she made a gift of it to her friend."

"The friend wouldn't say. Authorities were close to an arrest when the boyfriend died in a car accident. Shortly afterward Emily disappeared. Nobody has seen her since, until she showed up here."

"She mentioned having family in Argentina."

"Well, she may have been to Argentina, maybe not. Emily Boyd creates and re-creates herself."

"Emily Boyd?"

"Or Gail Braun, or Dana Greer, or Pamela Prescott and who knows what other aliases she's used."

"It doesn't sound like she did anyone harm who didn't deserve it."

"Those aren't questions for law enforcement," Inspector Lévesque said blandly.

"How did you identify her?"

"I'm not at liberty to share that information."

Inspector Lévesque once again leaned forward in his chair. "Thank you for your time, Mr. Walker." Then he stood and we shook hands. He opened the door and ushered me into the hall. "You'll be available if we have any more questions?"

"Of course. You have my address. Feel free."

I felt relieved to be finished with the interrogation. I turned to walk down the hall. I had taken a few steps when Inspector Lévesque's voice spoke again, "Did you get it?" He was holding his notepad.

I turned, confused. "Get what?"

"The book."

"No, I didn't. He told me he'd packed her things, and that she should call and make an appointment to come for them."

"Thanks, Mr. Walker."

"You're welcome."

I turned once again and as I opened the door at the end of the hallway Inspector Lévesque's voice stopped me again.

"What was the name of the book?"

I turned. "John Richardson's *Life of Picasso*." He wrote that down and waved me off with his pen. Inspector LÈvesque worried me. He watched too much television, or I did. I went home with a splitting headache.

The police ruled Alan's death a suicide. He had been under federal investigation for tax fraud and drug trafficking. Under new laws, the IRS had unearthed his offshore accounts and his worst fears were materializing. The federal apparatus was catching up with hacking techniques of the Melrose Maynards of the virtual world.

The note Alan Lansing left, written and signed in his distinctive handwriting, convinced authorities that at the end he had tried to make amends. They were especially impressed with his wish to bequeath a substantial trust to the destitute families of the corporations he'd helped to bankrupt. Authorities on several fronts were closing in and he knew it. Inspector Lévesque was able to conclude that under the stress of personal reversals Alan Lansing had taken his own life. The case was closed.

forty-five

Emily Schaffer, fugitive: it was hard to believe; how can you know about anyone? But I wasn't surprised; I'd seen something unusual in her. Women of an unlawful nature are far more interesting than men of the type: the renegade female has an allure that falls to men only after they're dead. I felt sorry for Bill Schaffer; he'd underestimated his wife's audacity and over-estimated her faith. Cruel consequences follow that sort of mis-judgment.

About a week after my interview with Inspector Lévesque, I heard about Emily's exit from a reliable witness. Old Moses, a twinkle in his eye, told of her escape. "She had a knapsack and the clothing she wore, nothing else," he said. "I saw her go. It was the night that man killed himself over at Rocky Point. Just be-fore sunup. She rowed out to Protestant Key; someone picked her up from there. You won't find her soon, my guess." A guess as good as any the Feds had.

I saw Inspector Lévesque on another occasion shortly after the findings on Alan's suicide were made public. We happened to sit next to each other one morning during breakfast at Capt'n Henry's, a popular local restaurant on the docks. "If Mr. Lansing hadn't left a note before he killed himself, we might have pursued other threads of evidence. Many people had good reason to see him dead." Inspector Lévesque didn't look at me when he said those words. He seemed to focus on a troll doll that Jimmy the cook kept on top of the cash register.

"I'm sure he wanted to undo all the evil he had done," I said, disingenuously solemn.

Inspector Levesque shrugged. "It served a better purpose to preserve his good intentions than to assume foul play. That call was mine, Mr. Walker." He stared at me. He wanted me to be sure we understood each other.

"By the way, I heard you made a big drug bust. A private yacht called *Destiny*. I've seen it in my travels."

"What do you know about it?"

"Nothing but what I read in the newspaper."

"Yes. It was a fortunate discovery. We have reason to believe the principals were tied in to Mr. Lansing. They'll be indisposed for a number of years."

Good, I thought.

part five

We shall not cease from exploration
And the end of all our exploring
Will be to arrive where we started
And know the place for the first time.
Through the unknown, remembered gate . . .

—T. S. Eliot

forty-six

In the fall of that year Mike Creato called with an invitation to join him and Rebecca on a sail from Fort Lauderdale to Bimini. The summer season in Edgartown was over and the Waco biplane had been hangared for the winter. They had migrated to Florida to spend the season on the boat Rebecca loved, their forty-foot sloop, *Aftermath*.

Johnny and Yarrow joined me; the three of us rode Jack Hibbard's Albatross on a flight from St. Croix to Miami. We drove from Watson Island up to Fort Lauderdale for a two-day cruise to Bimini.

Yarrow had been a great mate on our charters, and over the months she and Johnny had awakened to each other. They were planning to move in together. It was something I saw coming, and I was happy for them. They worked well as a couple: her independent nature brought something practical to his romantic inclinations, and his poetic temperament flattered her pride: he softened her and she toughened him.

We parked at the dock and I saw Mike wave from the deck of *Aftermath*. We walked to the slip, boarded, and stashed our bags below. The sky was clear and the salt air strong with the scent of the sea; the prosperous odor of fresh-cut grass was also in the air; the creosote planks of the dock smelled of tar and fish.

Mike started the engine and I jumped down, uncleated the spring line, stepped aboard again, and we backed out of the slip into the inland waterway, where we drifted past backyards of great estates, the Mediterranean, Mission, and Spanish homes that Floridians favor, stucco facades and barrel clay roof tiles in clusters of palm trees.

"A perfect day," Mike said, squinting in the glare of strong sun, bright on the water as we turned into the channel. "I'm glad you could make it."

The wind was moderate, out of the south. Mike set the mainsail and Rebecca unfurled the genoa; we held a broad reach making for the open ocean. Sailing has many sensations familiar to flying: soothing rhythms, latent menace; like the air, the ocean is something you feel in your soul; its mysteries veil the sublime.

Rebecca stood on the bow. Mike tightened the sheet. Once we got into open ocean the wind's velocity increased. We picked up a heading to Bimini, fifty miles away.

We dropped anchor in the harbor at Bimini before sunset, and after a delicious dinner on board, we took the dinghy into town for a pub crawl. The streets were full of day sailors and tourists from Florida. The six of us went from place to place, the honest bars by the docks with local charm. Mike was a good drinker of beer, and as time went on his eyes got glassy. Rebecca preferred marijuana; every once in a while she'd slip outside. When she came back her syntax was slightly puzzled and she laughed at almost everything and that made you laugh. Johnny drank rum, and his voice got louder as the night went on, or maybe the bars got louder and we were all yelling. I was nursing a chardonnay, feeling no pain. We had a table outside where you could see the boats in the harbor. The view was wonderful, but the service was abysmal, which is so often the case; I got up to get another glass of wine at the bar when someone tapped me on the shoulder from behind.

"Howdy, mate," the voice said.

I turned. It was Mitch Holden. I was incredulous. "Christ," I said. "How are you, Mitch?" We exchanged a look of pleasure that needed no explanation. "Why don't you join us? Johnny's here, and Yarrow's with us; you remember her."

"I'd like to, but I can't. I've got to go right now, but why don't you meet me here tomorrow and we'll have lunch. I'll bring you up-to-date."

"Everything all right?"

"Right as rain, mate. I'll see you tomorrow, then?"

"Sure."

"Just you. About one P.M."

I don't remember much about the rest of the evening. I remember lights and music and noise and talking, and Rebecca laughing, and Mike trying to tell a joke, forgetting the punch line, then spending the rest of the night trying to recall it, and Johnny and Yarrow kissing in dark corners of their own world. They were soberest at the end, and led us to the dinghy. I remember getting into the dinghy and seeing the lights of Bimini, and hearing far-off laughter, but that's all I remember until morning, when it all seemed like a dream.

I woke to the glare of sunlight, sprawled across pillows someone had arranged in the stern of *Aftermath*. The others were still sleeping in the staterooms when I went below to make coffee. My head was foggy, but my stomach was all right and my forehead didn't ache; all in all, I was none the worse for a roaring night. When the coffee was made I filled a mug and went topside to the stern again and sat on the pillows squinting in the bright morning sun. It felt good to be on a boat with someone else in command, where I had nothing to do but ride as a passenger.

The sun was hot on my face. Bimini looked peaceful, tranquil, an ideal beach village seen from a boat at anchor in the harbor. I was staring blankly without a thought in my head when I remembered Mitch.

When the rest of them finally resurrected I told Mike I was meeting someone for lunch and he said they planned to shop in town and go to the beach. We agreed to meet at the dinghy no later than 4:00 P.M. to begin sailing back in the late afternoon. After a breakfast of eggs and bacon and biscuits and Bloody Marys, we declared ourselves fit for shore duty, and off we went, the five of us happy as thieves.

I found the bar with little difficulty. I went in and the room was empty. The place smelled of liquor and cigarettes of the night before. Music was playing. A door was open behind a screen at the far wall. A television over the bar was channeled to CNN, with transcripts for the hearing impaired in subtitles while Roy Orbison sang "It's Over," his plaintive, ghostly tenor trilling on the strutting drumbeat of teenage despair. I took a seat and a barman came out from behind the screen and brought me a beer. I settled in, enjoying the darkness and emptiness and quiet, my eyes adjusting. Minutes later the door opened and a bright blade of light cut into the dark room: it was Mitch.

"Jason," he said, smiling expansively with that Australian charm, the way I remembered him in St. Croix.

"Have a seat," I told him. "So what in hell is up with you?" I said.

"A lot, laddie, to be honest: I'm in love."

"Is she real or imagined?"

"She's more real than I could have imagined. It's been in the works for a while."

"Do I know her?"

"As a matter of fact, you do. She'll be along in a moment."

The words were no sooner out of his mouth when the door opened again, and in from out of the same blinding blade of light walked Emily Schaffer. She was dressed in khaki shorts and a khaki safari shirt with a rose-colored scarf, her finely pronounced features beautiful as ever, her eyes full of cheer and amusement.

"Jason," Emily Schaffer said. She embraced me and kissed me warmly.

"Life is full of surprises."

They both laughed.

"It's great to see both of you," I said.

"Take the table over there." Mitch indicated a table in the corner. "I'll get Emmy a drink."

Emily and I went over to the table and sat down. "I know you're wondering what happened, why I left so suddenly."

"I'm always open to a good story."

"Ten years ago I did a favor for a friend that got me into trouble with the law."

"I know about it. The federal marshal on St. Croix told me."

"Then you know I've been a fugitive."

"Yes."

"Alan Lansing recognized me and turned me in to the Feds."

"When did you know him?"

"Alan Lansing knew me as Pamela Prescott twelve years ago, before the kidnapping incident. I met him when he came to Buenos Aires to do business with my father. My father was a rancher in Argentina for many years. Fifteen years ago he sold the ranch and bought an importing firm. That firm was eventually taken over by a holding company Alan Lansing controlled. He raped the company. His promises left us virtually penniless. It destroyed my father; he killed himself."

"I'm sorry."

"Alan Lansing killed my father as surely as if he had pulled the trigger himself. I went to St. Croix to settle a score."

I leaned into her space. "He did the job himself, as it turned out."

She moved closer and met me head-to-head.

"I was there when you played your game of Russian roulette. I had gone there to kill him myself."

Mitch came back to the table with Emily's rum and put down another beer for me. She must have seen a stab of fear in my eyes. This was not a subject I wanted to discuss.

"I'm not sure about anything that happened that night," I said, leaning back in my seat.

She reached across the table and took my hand affectionately between hers, like lovers do when they want to reassure emotional mistrust.

"I watched a man commit suicide, Jason, a man who deserved to die. And he left a note that tried to right wrongs, an uncharacteristic act of contrition." She looked me squarely in the eye. "We'll never know why he did that."

"Let dead dogs lie," I said.

"You just wrote Alan's epitaph." Mitch put his arm around Emily.

"What about the other issues?" I said.

Mitch leaned forward to speak confidentially. "Emmy and I set sail early that morning and disposed of your friends straightaway. I chummed the waters as we went and tossed the bodies overboard; a nice school of sharks had corpse du jour for breakfast. As far as the cash goes, *Threshold* is a floating retirement fund. The bills are sealed into the hull under a new layer of fiberglass. When Em and I get across the Pacific I'll call you. We're leaving this afternoon. I've already made arrangements with a bank in Hong Kong. The deeds to three luxury apartments will be waiting for us when I deliver the cash. Tell Johnny. I'll contact you both when we arrive." He winked at Emily and smiled at me. "The cruising life for us." He turned to find the bartender. "Bring us another round, will you, mate? And a menu."

forty-seven

In the year since Alan's death, Charlotte had discovered new strength and confidence. Her portfolio now combined Alan's remaining assets with her own; her philanthropy had gone a long way to right the wrongs of her husband. Besides establishing charitable instruments, she'd had great success investing strategically in a bear market.

Charlotte's relationship with money was like a sculptor's relationship with clay; her approach to investing grew from enjoyment, not avarice, and as I told her once, if you're going to unearth unsuspected native capacities, a Midas touch isn't the worst discovery to make about yourself. She was a very wealthy woman.

I, by comparison, was nearly broke. Paper wealth of millions had formed into a paper plane and launched itself out of my accounts. I didn't really mind; I was doing what I wanted to do, and of course there was the promise Mitch made to Johnny and me, but I didn't count on that. My approach to financial comfort is to have enough cash on hand so that whatever you want to do seems free. I have never defined myself with bank statements because money has no qualities, which is why there is always something a little ridiculous about people who measure their worth by it. My wealth was gone, but life was richer than it had ever been.

Charlotte loved the water as much as I did; living in Larchmont alone had rejuvenated her; vibrancy in her personality had replaced the depression she was dying from when we'd met. When she asked me to visit I didn't know how it would be between us.

She handed me a glass of wine and looked at me with speculative eyes. "I think I know you pretty well," she said playfully, like a schoolgirl charming a boyfriend.

I parried: "What do you think you know?"

She smiled. "I know that in many ways you're fearless, maybe even a little crazy." She sipped her tea, watching my response.

"I'm flattered."

"Thoughtful, deliberate, accomplished, naïve in some ways—"

"—I'm less flattered."

"You're a bit callow, especially when it comes to women. You don't understand love particularly."

That hurt. "Go on."

"Money doesn't mean much to you—so you say—but that's a half-truth to console ambivalence about it. You enjoy the power and freedom of money."

"I'm at ease with it or without it."

"Your sensibility is attracted to forms of enlightenment, specifically artistic expression, but you weren't brought up to it."

"Is anyone?"

"You have an autodidact's reverence for learning that's touching and pure; secretly you feel superior to almost everyone."

Distant thunder rumbled. I noticed a wasp near the rafter. It hovered for a moment, swooped across the room, out of sight: I thought, Alan again, in a meager reincarnation.

"With flying you live in the world; with writing you live in your dreams. You're lucky; you've uncovered an artistic imagination and discovered it to be compelling. Your days have become a flight over oceans and islands; your nights are your room and a typewriter and a committed will; you are quite happy with the life you've made for yourself, its serenity and challenge."

"It works for me."

She paused again, looked me straight in the eye. "Did I miss anything?"

"Nagging doubt, performance anxiety."

She laughed. "But you have the life you imagined for yourself."

"A curse of answered prayers."

"You don't believe that."

"Maybe not. And your point in telling me these things is . . . ?"

"Isn't it obvious?"

"Is it?"

"I'm in love with you, Jason."

There was a pause; she queried my expression. Finally I said, "I thought you were going to say good-bye gracefully."

"Did you really?" Humor faded from her face, forming into a sudden deep, scrutinizing maturity.

"We need each other," she said, with great conviction, and then paused to find her argument. "We have the same fears."

I went across the room to the vertical window facing the Sound. "What do you fear?" I asked.

"Uncertainties," she said, "limitations, that life goes on and

I might not be the person I want to be or do the things I want to do."

"No one can predict what will happen next in an uncertain world," I said. I was noticing the wind on the water, its face of curlews and foam. "Life imposes limitations."

"What's important to you, Jason?"

"People," I said, "good people." I turned to see her. "You're important to me. As I get older I feel a kind of vague dread, like a child's first sense of death after a terrifying nightmare about time."

"Could that be loneliness?"

That made me smile. "It could be."

"Should I doubt your ability to love me?" She was serious now, and truthful.

I turned from the storm on the Sound and smiled at Charlotte and came back to the table.

"I'm thinking of something Mitch told me once. We imagine other people; I'm able to imagine you. Imagination is our special gift, and it has no boundaries."

Charlotte blushed. "I remember when you said that happiness is not part of nature's plan, and that no one's entitled to it. I think that's true." She moved closer to me and her eyes were very honest. "Do you know what you want, Jason?"

I took her hand and there was a moment between us that commanded elements: thunder like falling timber crashed the silence. We got up from the table and went to the window to look out. Purple clouds moved fast above the white waves, bringing the sweet freshwater smell of the advancing storm. Rain began to sweep across the channel, and the sky grew darker. We watched it with the thrill of giddy children.

In the beginning we are strangers to the world and to the world's strangeness, but in time we grow accustomed to the idea of the sun; we accept the moon and seasons, even that it all ends; in time life's strangest aspects no longer seem peculiar.

I was always hungry, searching for larger experience. But once you have a certain amount, it's a surprise to learn how near and abundant real riches are, and how the great adventure is the one you've been having all along. Charlotte and I stood together at the window; we wanted the storm; we waited for lightning; we wanted the brilliant flash and its thunder for that sober sense of life that storms bring.

And it did come; a huge fork lit the dark sky and unleashed an earsplitting sound resonating the beginning of something or the end of everything. Charlotte squeezed my hand and I had that emotionally driven sense of moving backward into the future, riding the elastic living moment, gorgeous, electric, vibrant, and shining; we had wandered alone through winding paths made from childhood dreams, and as adults held on to those dreams through mistake and misgiving, until against long odds we found each other.

acknowledgments

The novelist in anyone is born in the dark. The struggle to grow and find a way to light with your work is an adventure as great as any epic. Monsters and demons lurk in the shadows; villains thwart you; knaves upset your peace of mind. There are others, though, who steadfastly help lead you to the path away from doubt. Without the unflagging support of the following individuals, this novel would not have found its shine: Dana Giusio, Eric Raab, Tom Doherty, Neal Bascomb, Byrd Leavell III, Michelle Tessler, Kathy Green, AnneAdare Wood, Ingrid Proescher, Joe Waxberg, Sue Casey, and Gail Fly. I'd like to offer special thanks to my editor, Bob Gleason, and to my longtime agent, friend, and fellow flyer, Michael V. Carlisle.